Just City

Olga Tymofiyeva

For more information: www.olga-tymofiyeva.com

just.city.book@gmail.com

Contents

To my parents, Liudmyla and Viktor,
who gave me everything

Chapter 1

I focus on the wall calendar above my grandmother's desk. September 1—the day to pitch startup ideas for the New Entrepreneur Incubator, the most prestigious incubator in San Francisco and all of the Bay Area. It's just three months away. My friend Jack and I are going in together, and it's going to be epic. At least that's what I tell Jack. I don't mention that I'm a bit nervous that we may fail.

I've always liked inspecting Grandma's study: rows of bookshelves, a dozen brain models on them—not surprising for a Professor of Neuroscience and Experimental Philosophy. Grandma sits at a large desk, finishing a video chat with one of her students. On the opposite wall is a large painting of a beautiful young woman with deep brown eyes. She is sitting at a table, holding a small marionette that appears to be a replica of herself. "MY FREE WILL"—the title is printed on a small white shield in the corner of the painting. I imagine myself moving my body by pulling invisible strings to accomplish things, driven by my willpower. I can do anything I want if only I put my mind to it. I reflect on my school successes and how my life has been a solid game so far and will be even better soon. I feel the power. I imagine being recognized at parties as one of the "top 10 entrepreneurs under the age of 25" and feel an adrenaline rush.

Grandma sounds enthusiastic, praising her student on Zoom. She catches my look and mouths, "I am almost done." I whisper back, "No problem," and keep looking at different objects in the study. I notice a blue sticker on the back of the computer monitor that seems to be new, "I BELIEVE IN GOD." Wait. I misread that; it reads, "I BELIEVE IN GOOD, the Humanist Society." That makes more sense. Grandma, who is a younger sister of my mom's late mother, is the only person in my family who admits she's an atheist.

Is my dad a believer? He's definitely a believer in hard work. He had several successful businesses and now he has a hydroponic farm near LA. Mom helps him there. Dad mentioned having a job for me there again the last time we talked. Man, I would NOT want that. Depending on Dad for work would mean depending on him for everything. He says it's just a backup option, but I don't think he believes I can be successful with my startup.

I know our startup idea is good, but the part that worries me is the $10,000 of our own pre-seed funding—*per founder*—that we need to enter the competition. That's why I'm here today. Grandma knows I'd rather not take money from the family. Yesterday, right after I was rejected from the paid summer internship that I'd been counting on, she called and said she had an idea.

When Grandma ends her call, I jump right in. "What's the brilliant idea?" I'm both doubtful and hopeful that whatever she suggests will not involve my dad's help. My dad only values work if you do it all on your own. Asking for his help would be admitting I've already failed, and I didn't come to San Francisco to be a loser.

Grandma looks upbeat. Her gray hair is in an immaculate bun, as always. She is petite and slender, sitting in her armchair with perfect posture. "Tell me, Nathan, if you were to create a truly just society, what would it look like?"

"A truly just society?" I wonder what this has to do with her idea and feel a bit irritated but decide to play along, hoping for a solution that will get me the money I need. I think for a second. "Well, those who work hard, who have talent and achieve things through their effort, should have stuff, and power." I feel a little proud of my off-the-cuff answer. I think about the Silicon Valley megastars who put in tons of work and talent, about the billionaire entrepreneur Peter Thiel (whom Jack admires) and feel that a just society is where they can shine, unlike some archaic dictatorship or something. And maybe I'll make it too, one day.

"Hmm, meritocracy."

"Meritocracy? Is that what you wanted to talk to me about?" I wish Grandma would just get to the point.

"Our videogame is ready," she says with a big smile.

"Oh, that's awesome!" The big project Grandma has been working on for several years is, of course, not a normal videogame—no boosting cars or creating block-shaped cities. She says it's the first online multiplayer virtual reality game "rooted in political philosophy." I'm really happy for her, especially because I thought the project had died. When she started the project, she tried collaborating with some professors in my Computer Science department at SF State, but then she switched to working with Berkeley guys. Grandma's Magnus University and our university never seemed to get along at the leadership level. She hasn't talked about the project in a while. But honestly, I think her research is too abstract, like that trolley car dilemma—which she can discuss for hours with her philosopher friend Mark—where you must decide whether to divert the trolley and save the lives of five railroad construction workers but let one worker down the side track die. I don't know how practical this research is. Like, really, what is it for? Jack once told a joke that mathematics is the second-cheapest department at any college because all you need is a pencil, paper, and a wastebasket. Philosophy is the cheapest because you only need a pencil and paper. I never told Grandma this joke, of course. It would be too much to imply that her work output is trash.

Chapter 2

A narrator describes the premise of *Just City*. "The veil of ignorance is a powerful idea introduced by philosopher John Rawls as part of the social justice theory. It is a thought experiment designed to ensure that all the rules and laws of society are created in a way that is fair and just for everyone. Under the veil of ignorance, no one knows which societal position they will fill, their class, gender, race, or creed, whether they will be born into wealth or not, what they will be good or bad at, or be in a position to achieve. The experiment invites thinkers to decide 'under the veil' what rules should govern society. It is postulated that only then can one truly appreciate the morality of an issue from all angles."

So apparently, I won't know who I am in society when I make up the rules of *Just City*, and therefore, I won't know how those rules will affect me until they are made up. Interesting. It shouldn't be a problem. There should always be an optimal, reasonable solution, and I pride myself on my analytical skills. I click on "Start Round 1."

The whole screen becomes dark, and a pair of dice rolls. An avatar appears in the top right corner, but its head is covered with a scarf I can't see through—the "veil of ignorance," I assume. Who am I under this scarf? What if I'm a woman?

It doesn't matter; if I play smart, I'll get the results I want.

The narrator announces that I've been assigned new characteristics which I won't be able to see yet. From this unbiased position, I'm expected to decide on the rules and regulations of *Just City* before finding out who I am and actually playing the round.

I am guided into a virtual room with a massive panel that has dozens of sliders. I am asked, by adjusting the sliders, to decide on the laws and regulations of *Just City* that will be applied to me in this round of the game: taxation, wages, health insurance policy, unemployment insurance, infrastructure, education policy, environmental policy, rights of minorities, laws on abortion, euthanasia, gun control, etc. Okay, abortion laws, euthanasia... that's a lot to think about. I feel like skipping all this stuff and moving on to the game, at least for the first round. Wait, high taxation—right—Jack always says that Michael Jordan had to give away over a third of his proceeds from ticket sales; that's basically forced labor. No way. I drag the tax slider down and leave the rest of the sliders in the default positions that represent the current U.S. situation, which I think is pretty good and fair.

I click "done" and music starts playing. The music sounds dramatic, and so does the narrator saying, "It is time to lift the veil of ignorance."

———◦———

I look down at my hands: white male. A mirror appears in front of me. I am a tall, athletic, good-looking man in his thirties. The list of characteristics in the info corner indicates gender, race, parents' social class, immigration status, physical and mental health, attractiveness, physical fitness, sexual orientation, and talents. No radical change for me: I'm not a woman, not gay, not of a different race. I feel a bit relieved. The rules of the game state that it's all about acquiring as many "well-being points" as possible by pursuing "life tasks:"

1. Find a job in *Just City*.
2. Find a partner
3. Engage in leisure activities and hobbies.

My current assigned situation shows me how I can earn these points. I, apparently, just quit my well-paying job in advertising, so I'll have to find a new job. I also have to find a wife/girlfriend. My hobby is cartoon drawing, which is sweet because I like sketching in real life. It seems I'm very good at it, and I have a blog and newsletter with my artwork. I can even read some hilarious samples of my work, like the one about a doctor discovering that his liberal patient was so open-minded that his brain fell out. Ha!

After reading about my character's life situation, I step outside my virtual house and end up in a town center with stores, banks, and museums around the perimeter. The area reminds me of Union Square, a gigantic and modernized version, with palm trees, people walking around and sitting outside cafés. Instead of square, it's round, with streets radiating from the center in all directions like rays. The sky is bright blue, and everything is lit with sunlight. In the middle of the square stands a statue of Lady Justice, blindfolded and holding a scale and a sword.

From what I understand of the rules, while many characters are preprogrammed, you also interact with real people whenever other players are online. The interaction is possible regardless of the choices other players made in their version of *Just City*. I really like that you can meet with real-life friends in a virtual hangout room by using their game IDs. I text my ID to the guys and tell them to meet me in the game once they start playing.

Since playing the game is limited to two hours a day, I decide to research the job market of *Just City* and learn how to find a romantic partner right away. I want to save the second hour for when the gang has joined.

Across the town center, I see a tall building with an "Indeed Jobs" sign. I approach the building and get access to a screen with a job browser. As I browse the list of job openings, and re-read the rules in detail on the side, I have the genius idea of searching for a job as a cartoonist. This will kill two birds with one stone: job and hobby. Indeed, there is a great demand for my talent as a cartoonist. I send out applications to potential sponsors for my freelance work. I know this round--well, this life--can last for up to a week, but if I accomplish goals faster, I get bonus points for speed.

After my first hour, I take a break and go for an evening run before my friends meet online at 10 p.m. I think about how finding a relationship works in the game and the possibility of hooking up with Jocelyn—in the game, I mean, not in real life.

Or maybe both.

Jocelyn, Jocelyn, Jocelyn. The blonde beauty is hard not to think about. I dreamed about her a couple of times after she broke up with her much older lawyer boyfriend, whom she dated for several years. I think she likes me too, or at least finds me handsome. Once, I was wearing a new outfit--an orange shirt with black patterns like those on Japanese knives with onyx pants--and I was having a good hair day. She said I could be a model. Would she agree to marry me in the game? My character is pretty awesome. The game also calculates a compatibility score for potential partners, which will affect the number of points. What if she is a man? Come on, I have to see her character first anyway. I can't help but picture the actual Jocelyn in a wedding dress. No, I don't think anything like that would ever happen in real life. She is fun, sexy, super smart, and more of a rational type than sweet and kind. But since I'm rational, my long-term girlfriend should probably complement me rather than be too similar.

At 10 p.m., we all finally meet in the game. We enter the same virtual hangout room by using our IDs. I can't believe it. Jack is a kind of Elon Musk type, a mega-entrepreneur. Man, it's too fitting. Adam is a woman, a technical translator—nice, and Jocelyn is a young middle school teacher—how cute. Because I had a head start, I explain my understanding of the game's rules. I think I can maximize my score if we all cooperate.

"It looks like working with people you know in real life is the best option, especially due to the speed bonus. For example, if Jack employs Adam at his company, it can boost Jack's score and fulfill Adam's job task," I tell them.

As Jack checks if he can (and wants to) offer Adam a job, I secretly run a check under my profile for the compatibility score between Jocelyn and me.

"Okay dude, it looks like it will give me a couple of points," Jack tells Adam, who seems pleased with the idea. "Let's do the interview now. We're supposed to go through some formalities according to the instructions. Hang out again tomorrow night at 10 with the rest?"

"Sounds good," I reply. "Jocelyn and I have to go through some formalities too."

"What?" Jocelyn's cute character steps back.

"Oh, yeah." I smile. "Will you marry me?" I pause intentionally for a dramatic effect. "Seriously, it will give us both a thousand points. You can check yourself. Our fit score is 98 percent. Very hard to top."

———◦———

The next day, Jocelyn and I get virtually married. The City Hall ceremony is minimalistic and not followed by a honeymoon or anything like that, unfortunately. The life task of finding a partner is completed, and our characters move on, but I can't stop thinking about it. Over the course of the week, all of us keep playing daily for two hours, and I call Jocelyn "my wife" whenever we all meet in the hangout room. My strategy to turn my character's hobby into a job pays off ridiculously well. With the low taxation I chose, my well-being points climb to three thousand in just a few days. I can't help thinking it will be the additional amount in dollars I will receive for the study participation. When interacting with other players, I can see their points, and they can see mine. The comparison is consistently in my favor, even with the gang. My score is a few hundred points higher than Jack's. Nice. Jack's character is super-rich and easily fulfills the job and hobby tasks (exploring the Galapagos Islands), but his partner-finding has been challenging. I told him to marry Adam, and he told me to go to hell.

Chapter 3

On Saturday, I meet with Jack in-person, and we go to a startup meetup where aspiring entrepreneurs can learn to pitch their ideas to investors. It's a forty-minute walk downtown, and I enjoy the chilly but sunny morning.

"Dude, the game—seriously, perfect timing!" Jack is wearing sunglasses, but I know he is squinting because it's the way he usually smiles.

I grin. It's usually Jack who gets us into cool stuff like this, like that gig with the new social network testing he found recently. I can't remember the name of it now, but it was so awesome to be able to be part of the initial platform. However, this time it's me who found this game, and even though I know we all only hang out together because of Jack, I feel important.

The meetup takes place in a café in the financial district near the Tenderloin, a famously sketchy part of the city.

We walk past an old wheelchair tipped over on the sidewalk. A homeless dude sleeps right in front of it, as if he fell out of the chair, crawled under some dirty blankets, and passed out. The scene inevitably prompts Jack to talk about his startup idea.

"So, I checked, and the idea is brand new. Our chip-traceable shopping carts for supermarkets will prevent the homeless from constantly stealing the carts and building their miserable existence inside them." Jack sounds confident, and I like the vicarious feeling of confidence.

"All those homeless shelters and programs," Jack continues, "for nothing—money down the drain. They just want to stay like this. They don't want to work."

It makes me think I would find a way out of homelessness and not stay in that situation a day longer. Why don't they do anything? There is so much someone can do. If they would just apply a little effort, I'm sure they could live better lives. I would definitely find a job first, work hard to afford a place, and end my homelessness as soon as possible.

Yet sometimes I feel like giving money to the homeless. Maybe it's my mom's influence or something. But I never do. It would be so irrational. Jack says that giving money to beggars only decreases their motivation to do anything. Has anyone ever seen a homeless person receive money and then stop being homeless? Some would find Jack's speeches a little cold, but I think he is just super rational.

We cross the street at a crosswalk, watching as a black teenager pulls a trashed pizza box from a garbage can, opens it, and puts it back—probably empty.

We keep talking about the startup. Jack did all the calculations and I trust him. Am I super enthused about the idea? Maybe not, but a startup needs to grow and make money, and I trust Jack's analytical skills. Not only is he majoring in economics, but he is also a genius—literally.

I met Jack when I was 17, in the Geniuses Club—a high school extracurricular activity for future leaders and innovators. He was included because he has an IQ of 170. I've never tested my IQ, but I know it's nowhere near that. I'm smart and hard-working, but those IQ geniuses are like gods.

The Geniuses Club is where we all met: Adam, Jocelyn, Jack, and I. I was there based on my grades and extraordinary coding skills, Jocelyn for grades and musical talent, and Adam as a chemistry genius. Jack's IQ was his in. Jack and I became friends first, and we didn't start hanging out with Adam and Jocelyn until later. Jack and I clicked because of our logical approach to things.

I remember the day I was supposed to lead a discussion regarding new club member candidates. After one semester of membership, everyone rotated into the role of the President, and it was my turn. Two of the candidates' resumes were pretty straightforward (and my suggestion was *not* to accept them), but one was slightly different. This guy had a pretty good knowledge of the law and achievements in mock trials, but he was not at the extraordinary level the Geniuses Club membership requires. Why were we even talking about this candidate, then? Well, he was blind. I had prepared my arguments, and once everyone was at the table, I started the discussion. I presented my opinion that we should not include him in the club. I said that what he achieved while being blind was pretty remarkable, but our club was supposed to be for future leaders and innovators, and we wanted only the best. I asked, "Wouldn't you want the person handling your case in the future... whatever that case is... surgery or a court defense, to be the top specialist in absolute terms?" The club members supported my decision, and Jack later complimented my argument regarding the new candidate.

"We are not a charity organization," he added.

It meant a lot to me.

Jack and I have become much closer friends since then. Our shared motto is, "You've got to be rational."

Jack often adds, "You are either a wolf or a sheep."

We teamed up and had all of our club proposals supported, thanks to playing smart together. It was an awesome time overall, even though I later got removed from my role as the President due to an anonymous complaint by one of the members about my budget mismanagement. Some loser from the club told our sponsor that I bought an unnecessary ultrawide, curved "gaming" monitor, although we had all agreed upon its purchase beforehand. I still don't know who did it. That was quite a disappointment, but my overall time in the club was excellent, mainly due to the fun Jack and I had. The prospect of having a startup together sounds even more fun.

We pass by another café where Adam and Jocelyn often hang out with the other medical students, and what do you know, the two are walking down the street toward us. They notice us and smile. They know we have our meetup and are about to walk past us. At the last moment, I stretch out my arm like a road barrier and catch Jocelyn at the waist level but let go of her immediately. This makes her spin around, and I hear her exclaim, "Dude!" as we all continue passing by each other. I know she is blushing. I think I'm finally going to ask her out.

<hr />

We arrive at the meetup and see that most regulars are already there. As Jack and I get drinks, we chat with the café owner, who always accommodates our group. He says that the screen for our activities is ready. I wonder what we are using it for today. We weren't told to prepare any pitches.

Today's surprise guest is not an entrepreneur but an improv theater teacher. He announces with a big smile that we will be doing "PowerPoint Karaoke"—we will be asked to improvise with slide decks for random startup pitches. People have to pitch in pairs, in front of everyone, without preparation.

Yikes! This sounds scary and a little bit exciting at the same time. But mostly scary. I imagine making a fool of myself in front of Jack, and everyone else, by going completely blank. A cold feeling spreads in my feet. I look at Jack, trying not to show my nervousness, and see his totally chill face and crossed arms. We look at each other and smile. One smile is real and confident, while the other is fake and nervous (mine). I'm jealous of Jack's calm. Well, what can I do? Keep faking being calm the whole time and hope it works out.

A dozen teams form, and Jack and I name our team "Rationals—get ahead." The improv teacher writes the twelve team names on the blackboard that's hanging on the wall. We are number nine, so I feel like we'll have enough time to observe the others and mentally prepare.

The improv teacher loads the first collection of slide decks and says, "I'm now going to use my random number generator app to see which team goes first." With his wide, annoying grin, he announces, "Rationals. The stage is yours!"

I look at Jack. He seems content with us going first. He even has his signature smirk on his face. I take a deep breath and pretend to be excited. "Power pose... power pose"— I recite presentation tips in my head and try to spread my shoulders and straighten my posture.

The rest is a bit of a blur, but a fantastic roller-coaster kind of a blur. Slide decks of all sorts of random startups appear one after another. Marijuana delivery startup, AI mattress startup, exercise app, home water quality control startup... Jack and I take turns switching at every slide. "When was the last time you got a good night's sleep?" Jack would ask the audience, then share confidently and convincingly the stats on sleep, almost without looking at the slide. I would jump in at the slide transition, announcing to everyone that we have a solution—an Artificial Intelligence mattress! As I speak, I grow more and more confident, seeing all eyes on me, on us, and feeling that we have the audience. Several times, when I realize I don't have ideas for a slide, Jack reads my mind and jumps in. Once I even do the same when Jack, with both hands, theatrically gestures to me during his slide. I successfully take over, feeling proud I could help him out. People applaud and cheer and laugh. Two young women who are new to the meeting and appear to be friends are beaming at us.

Man, Jack and I rock!

As we are wrapping up our presentations and listening to the praise from the improv teacher, I look into the mirrors on the wall behind the screen. I find myself so damn good-looking. It is interesting how I really like the way I look on some days and on others, I don't at all. It's the same body and the same face. Today I'm a star: a grownup, attractive man with outstanding academic achievements and a bright future, who secretly still feels like a child inside. Is it something everyone feels about themselves? I look at Jack's reflection. I doubt he ever feels like he is still a child inside. He probably never felt like that even when he was a child. There is this mysterious seriousness about him. He looks fantastic, a different type from me. I know I'm more of a sweet kind, and he has a "darker," more masculine style—kind of powerful. Luckily, girls usually prefer either one or the other type. Although I know it hasn't always been that easy for Jack.

I remember back when we were in the Geniuses Club, we were hanging out at his parents' place, and I saw this photo of an obese child. I was shocked to find out Jack was a fat kid. I thought it must have been a different kid—his brother or a cousin, but it was him. He was seriously bullied for his weight. But when he was 15, he decided to read up on and try weight loss programs. By the time we met in the Geniuses Club, he looked terrific. It's amazing what determination, intelligence, and hard work can do. I'm lucky to have him as my startup partner and friend. We might actually become famous "unicorns!" And the excitement of pitching for our startup will probably be a million times stronger than what I feel today.

After we sit down, all the other teams present in turns. I enjoy some of the presentations, but I know—everyone else knows it, too—that Jack and I were the best. Man, we were on fire!

When we leave the meetup, I say, "Jack, you totally had my back." He smirks and I continue, "I have a very good feeling, we'll get the money we need through the game and nail the Incubator application." Jack nods in approval.

I hesitate slightly but then ask, "Do you ever feel like you are still a child inside?"

"What do you mean?"

"You know, like you are officially a grownup, but in reality, you are just pretending. Like you are still nervous about things, still trying to figure things out?"

"Is that what you feel?"

"A little bit," I reply. "But I can't wait to be able to tell my parents in the fall that I'm a startup cofounder and part of the most prestigious New Entrepreneur Incubator."

"That does sound grownup indeed."

I look at Jack's face to see if he is being ironic, but he seems to mean it, and I'm relieved. Even though he didn't tell me he shared my feeling about being like a child, I feel closer to him. I can't wait to start the next round of *Just City* on Monday. Man, this is so cool.

Chapter 4

Monday. The next round of *Just City* starts today. I did really well in my previous life. My 4,500 points shine in the top left corner of the screen.

The upbeat Twenty-something song plays again, and I feel it's about me. After all, I'm twenty-one and full of energy and potential. The dice roll again. I decide to save time and leave the rules and regulations of *Just City* as they were in the first round. I think they are pretty good. The veil of ignorance is lifted.

I am a 17-year-old kid, white, with brown hair. I look slender, but athletically built, in some ways similar to how I looked when I was 17. The assigned situation is bizarre. I am accused of a rape and murder I didn't commit. This sudden change in the mood of the game totally confuses me. I didn't expect it to be exactly like the last round, but I saw the gang's lives too, and none of them were anything close to this craziness.

But something else freakish is going on. My control over the actions of my avatar is limited. I cannot even click on the job search section.

I don't even get to visit the square with the statue of Lady Justice. Instead, I find myself in an interrogation room. The detective is asking me about my uncle and a woman who was at my uncle's place. I respond according to the info on my character. "Yes, our house is next to my uncle's house, and I often help him with the yard..." When it comes to whether I was in my uncle's house on a particular night, I say, "No," but... what the heck... the game mutes my answer, and instead, my character, in a pre-recorded male voice, says, "Yes."

I feel pressure in my throat.

Out of control, my character continues, "She was tied to the bed, and my uncle asked me if I wanted to go next."

I'm so shocked that I press pause and take my VR goggles off. What the heck? The script clearly says I didn't do it! And I clearly said no! I pace around the room for a minute, then put the goggles back on. The interrogation continues. Sometimes the answers I say come through, contradicting what I unwillingly admitted to when talking to the detectives a moment ago. But then my speech is overtaken again, and I quietly tell the detectives the horrible details of the rape and murder... How she was tied to the bed... I even make a schematic drawing of how her throat was slit and her body burnt in the backyard bonfire. I'm being taken away by the guards and find myself in jail. It's pretty dark, and I look at a tiny window at the very top of the wall. This is a bunch of nonsense.

A guard comes in and asks if I want to talk to my mother on the phone.

"Mom," I say to my mother.

"Son!"

"I'm in jail," I say and attempt to explain what happened, but I lose control of my character's speech again. However, this time the algorithm of the game tells a different story for me, no longer saying that I did it.

"I don't know what happened, Mom."

"Did you do it?" she asks.

"What?"

"Did you do what they say, with your uncle, to that woman?"

"No! Of course not," the game voice replies for my character.

"No?"

"No, Mom."

"Why on earth did you say that you did it?"

"I don't know."

"How did you know all those details?"

"I don't know.""What do you mean you don't know?"

"I guessed."

"You guessed?! You don't guess such things! What do you mean you guessed?"

"You know. I guessed. I do it with my homework all the time."

Silence.

"I know..." Mother says.

I can't take it anymore, and I pause the game. It's not like I'm playing anyway. I don't understand what's going on. Why don't I have control over my character anymore? And who would do something like that, admit to a crime they didn't commit?

Disturbed and angry, I go across the street to my grandma's. It's past 7 p.m., so she should be home.

I ring the doorbell.

"Hello?" she says through the security speaker.

"Grandma, what's up with your stupid game?"

She slowly begins, "Oh, I see, Nathan. Please come in."

I can't hold back my words when she opens the door.

"The *Just City* game is rigged. I couldn't talk, my character would just say what he wanted most of the time, and the whole thing sucks. I confessed to this horrible crime I didn't do!"

As we head to the study, Grandma replies in an annoyingly calm voice, "Actually, we use a random generator, making the role assignment independent of who is playing. So, it's not rigged. As for you not being able to fully control your avatar in certain lives, that was in the introduction somewhere. This is our attempt to simulate how a person's cognitive abilities affect the decisions they make and show the consequences as they play out in life's game of chance. While most of the players' actions are controllable, we had to limit that in cases where diminished executive function is part of the character in a particular round."

"But it's bullshit. I am who I am, and I am good at the game. I had 4,500 points in the last round!"

"Great! I hope you chose rules allowing for a good public defender in this round."

"That's not funny, and no, I didn't! This game is a bunch of nonsense."

"It's actually not nonsense – the 1,500 scenarios and characters we programmed are largely based on real stories. Yours too. It's a famous case..."

"I would never say something so stupid!" I interrupt.

"I know, but the whole point is that you wouldn't say it if you were *you*. But you *would* if your genes and environment, every single cell in your brain, and every little event in your life happened the way they happened to him."

"No, I wouldn't."

"Look at this brain." She stands up and grabs one of the brain models from the shelf. "The orbitofrontal cortex had a tumor that made the owner of this brain a pedophile and a criminal, but he stopped being those things after the tumor was removed. Then he relapsed again after the tumor grew back. So yes, *you* wouldn't have done those things, but you *are* your brain, your connectome, which means the network of all the connections in your brain. Different brain, different connectome—different decisions. And you see, *you* didn't make your brain from scratch. You didn't choose it. Your brain now chooses things, true, but you didn't choose your brain. To put it nicely: *A man can do what he wants but not want what he wants.* Schopenhauer."

I frown, not knowing what to say. My breathing still feels heavy. The words "you didn't make your brain from scratch" don't sit well inside. I feel these words not only try to justify all the losers of the world but also attempt to take away everything I've been proud of. Can I be proud of anything at all if I'm not responsible for all my accomplishments? What's the point, then?

"Would you like to stay for dinner?" Grandma asks.

"Thank you, but I'd rather go."

I slowly eat dinner at home by myself, without even watching any shows. I keep thinking about what Grandma said. Suppose I am my brain, my connectome, which I didn't choose or make from scratch. Does it mean that I could have been entirely different, and none of that would have been my fault or my achievement? Does it mean that genes and environment determine not just my talents but even qualities like perseverance and being hard-working? No, it's nonsense! I don't believe this.

I don't want to believe this.

Chapter 5

The next day I continue playing the same round of *Just City*. My family is poor, and I can't make bail. My total score drops to 2,800 points because I am not making progress. But I know that the prospects are even worse. I need to find at least two character witnesses for my day in court. Asking AI-based or other real players seems useless because everyone wants something in exchange, and my character doesn't really have anything. So, I ping the gang by using their IDs and ask for a short VR meeting. Short, because that's all my character is allowed to have in jail.

Only Jocelyn and Jack seem to be playing right now, and we meet in the VR hangout room. I feel relief. Two witnesses should be enough. Jack's profile shows that he is the owner of *The Just City News*. He sees my profile, and his 60-year-old avatar excitedly says, "No way, you are the scandalous teenage psycho who murdered that woman..." He continues, "My news agency is all over the story!""Not murdered..." I reply, feeling like a child. Well, my avatar is 17, and Jack's is 60.

"Not murdered? But didn't you confess?" Jack asks.

"The game is stupid." I can't explain the whole thing because my time is running out. "Can you just..."

"Come on, suddenly the game is stupid?" Jack interrupts, as he is obviously on a roll this round.

"Guys, can you serve as my character witnesses?" I continue anyway.

"I'm not sure. Won't it cost us points?" Jack asks.

I didn't expect this reaction from Jack. He doesn't seem to understand. "Come on, I will hit rock bottom if they find me guilty... And because of the confession, my lawyer said strong character witnesses are my only chance."

"So, you confessed?" Jocelyn speaks for the first time. She is an auto mechanic in this round. Damn it, everyone is doing well in this round again! Except me.

"The game literally overrode me... It's a long story. I just need your testimonies..."

Jack interrupts. "Come on, it's a game. We have to think about ourselves. We team up if it benefits both of us, but you don't expect sacrifices, do you? We need some healthy egoism in the game."

Even though Jack says that we have to think about ourselves because it's a game, a memory of him commenting on the homeless comes to my mind. It's just my avatar going down, but what if I were in similar trouble in real life? How would Jack treat me?

"Doesn't seem to be only in the game for you, does it? It's not that much different in real life," I say.

"Are you saying I'm selfish? How is that any different from you? What do you do differently?" Jack's avatar looks stern. He barely pauses before continuing, "Well? Tell me more about how selfless you are. Unlike me..."

Suddenly the hangout room's light blinks, and I'm reminded with a message that my hangout capabilities are limited because I'm in jail.

I take the goggles off. I need a break. What *is* going on? Am I getting into a *loser mentality*? Has some stupid fake game character hijacked my brain? Fake game. Suddenly chills run down my spine. Grandma's words about the fact that my character and scenario are based on real events make me unable to swallow. Some boy out there went through exactly this. I wonder what happened to him in the end.

My thoughts are interrupted by Adam's text to the gang. He wants to meet in the *Just City* game, as he missed our last meeting. I go back to the game, unsure if my character will have the freedom to hang out again, and after about 10 minutes of trying, I manage to join the VR hangout room. I enter and see that Adam, Jack, and Jocelyn are already there. Jack's avatar occupies most of the screen since he is talking.

"...I am too selfish in the game AND in real life, apparently. And he is a saint."

I immediately press the "Exit the hangout room" button, as my ears and cheeks become hot in a flash. Did he see me? Maybe there's a chance he didn't. The bitterness about the things Jack just said about me behind my back strikes me. How could he do that? Jack and I have been much closer to each other than to Adam and Jocelyn, yet he says this to them. What if he always talks about me like that? I take the goggles off and go to the kitchenette to make tea. As the water starts to boil in the glass kettle, suddenly the termination letter of my presidency at the Geniuses Club flashes in front of my eyes. Noooo, that cannot be true. Nonsense. I start feeling nauseous from the thought that the anonymous complaint back at the Geniuses Club could have come from Jack. No, no, no.

I know he became the President right after me, and it played really well for his applications for the investment consulting internship. I remember feeling a little better because of that: At least something good came out of my presidency termination for Jack. It can't be that he actually did it.

I have a flashback of me sharing with Jack how upsetting it was that one of our own told the club's sponsor about the VR set... Especially because we *all* agreed upon it!

"Should I talk to everyone individually? Should I try to find out?" I remember feeling shocked by the termination.

"Do you really care that much? I thought you'd had a good run and had enough of the presidency." Jack was bringing me back to reality, which I found to be a genuine expression of friendship back then.

Suddenly our whole friendship appears to have been a fake.

Chapter 6

The next day I don't look forward to playing the game at all. The events my character is going through seem so dark and depressing. Of course, the guy whose life this scenario is based on had to wake up to it for real every morning. I don't want to imagine how scared he must have been.

But even more than my character's life, I don't want to think about whether Jack did what I think he did back in the Geniuses Club. So, I choose the lesser evil, put the VR goggles on, and continue the game. The court verdict is in, and I can't believe it. Guilty on all charges. Sentenced to life in prison. And since I didn't allocate any funding for an innocence program at the beginning of the round, my family doesn't have any money, and no kind, wealthy person is fighting for me, it's a done deal. My points for this round go to zero. I knew my overall score was going to drop drastically, but apparently, I get an additional penalty for hitting rock bottom! Even though I had 4,500 points from the last round, my total drops to a sad 409 points.

I feel devastated and overwhelmed by everything that has been happening. The dream of money for the startup —at least for my share—is fading, and so is my understanding of what kind of friendship Jack and I have. What am I supposed to do now? I reluctantly realize that I have to talk to Jack, at least about the money part.

I text Jack, asking him to meet in the game. I'm still not sure what to tell him. My avatar is still the teenager, now wearing an orange prison jumpsuit. I decide to start by confronting Jack about his unwillingness to help me, which resulted in me losing most of my points. He should at least care about that part because we both need the money.

"Thank you for your help, Jack," I say sarcastically when he finally shows up in the hangout room.

"Dude, it's just a game."

"A game? I won't get even close to $10K for our startup at this rate."

"Oh, enough of this whining. You can ask your parents for the money. Toughen up."

His comment about my parents makes me even angrier. He knows that I want to do it on my own.

Jack continues, "Besides, we agreed to help each other only if it benefits both characters. I don't want to be dragged down by your loser character."

This hits me personally. The boundary between the game characters and our real personas becomes blurry. Being my current character started to give me an idea of what it is like to be on the other side of us. Yes, *us*, because Jack and I are so similar in how we see other people's failures.

"Look, people don't choose to be in trouble." I try to defend my character.

"They choose what to do about it," Jack replies.

A picture of my grandma with the brain in her hand flashes in front of my eyes—her telling me how we don't choose our brain, don't make it from scratch. And all the decisions that follow... I raise my voice.

"No, they don't!" I'm a bit surprised at my own words and at the same time, feel convinced of what I'm saying. Earlier, I would never say something like this to Jack. Now, from inside a different person, I see and say it.

"Yes, they do!" Jack raises his voice too.

"Does a toddler decide what happens to him? Does it influence the rest of his life?" I think about the brain and free will but don't know how to express it.

"What a lame argument. Dude, have you overheated?"

I feel frustrated that he doesn't understand and doesn't want to listen. I hit where it might really hurt. "Did you choose to be a fat kid?"

Jack angrily replies, "Did I choose to f-ing read everything on weight loss programs and use willpower to lose 90 pounds in six months? Now to you, do you choose to grow up, stop being a sissy, and start to take responsibility for your actions? Or is it too much to ask of you?"

I told him how I feel like I'm still a child inside... I thought we were a team!

"Is it grown up to talk behind your friend's back and to file anonymous complaints to have him removed from the club presidency?"

Jack pauses. "Look," he says slowly and much quieter than before, "I never meant..."

He does not deny it. His tone makes it clear: HE DID IT!

"You bastard!"

I squeeze my controller and can't help throwing my hand forward. To my surprise, my character hits Jack's character, just like in fighter video games. I never used it here, and I didn't think this game would even have something like that. Jack punches me in return. My avatar falls back, with sound and everything. I stand up and start fighting as hard as I can—not because I know it's just a game but because I want to hit Jack hard. He throws a nasty punch to my face, and I use both hands to retaliate. I keep throwing punches and feel burning in my eyes. My vision becomes a bit blurry. I throw punch after punch, seeing scenes from my memory flash in front of my eyes. First, the presidency termination letter, then Jack talking behind my back to Adam and Jocelyn, but then scenes of all the people disadvantaged by their fate. The homeless man near the wheelchair Jack and I saw the other day, the hungry teenager, people who do not know any better, people suffering, people in misery flash in front of my eyes, filling me with pain and anger. Anger at Jack, as if all that suffering were his fault.

A sharp pain accompanies my next punch. Damn it, I hit the physical wall in my room as I moved too far from the armchair during the fight. The pain is excruciating, and I think my hand is probably bleeding. Jack is down, but he is about to get up. I exit the game and take the goggles off. Smeared blood on my fist and the controller brings me back into reality, which feels as weird as the game. I've never fought with Jack before. I wash my hands, grab my hoodie, and go for a run. It's getting dark, and I sprint, feeling like my throat is burning. I hate him. The thought keeps repeating itself with each footfall. *I Hate Him!*

I hate him for his betrayal in the Geniuses Club.

I hate him for not helping my character in the game.

I hate him for not listening and ridiculing my point about the lack of free will.

I hate him for not caring about me.

I. Hate. Him. For not caring about anyone other than himself!

I growl as I run.

I hate him... for the fact that he wasn't technically breaking our shared "rationality code" when he betrayed me. Play smart to get ahead. Did that say anything about caring for each other? Of course, it didn't.

I reach the bay and pause near the water, staring at the darkness interspersed by streetlight reflections. My hand lands on the little "tiger eye" rock I always carry in my pocket, my reminder to always be reasonable. I came up with it long before I met Jack.

I was 12, and I remember it clearly. There was a woman in the apartment next to ours, Silvia, whose brother Luc sometimes visited her.

That day I was home by myself, exploring the globe when the doorbell rang. I saw Uncle Luc in the peephole and opened the door. He asked me if my parents were home, and after I said they were away, he asked if he could come in and sit down to rest a bit. The way he was walking was funny, and the way he spoke was much slower than usual. He sat down on a chair and asked how my school was going. He then asked if I could help him. He needed some money for some medication. Tomorrow he'd receive his paycheck and give it back right away. He told me he was not feeling well without his medication. I felt sorry and went to my room to get the $25 my parents and Grandma gave me to buy a rock collection. When I brought the money to Uncle Luc, his eyes lit up. He was so grateful; he kept pressing the money to his chest and thanking me. He repeated that he would bring it back the next day and left. I felt so good, I felt like I really helped someone, like I was a grownup capable of helping others. It was a serious situation, and I helped. My mom always said it's important to help others. My mom and dad always praised me with the nicest words when I helped them or Grandma with chores or anything, even small things.

My parents came home that evening. I told them what happened, secretly expecting praise and admiration from my parents, but my dad suddenly became stern. He said that Uncle Luc was a lazy alcoholic who hadn't worked in years and that it was naive to expect him to give the money back to me. He probably spent the money on alcohol the minute he left the house. "You have to think and be reasonable before you do things like this. You have to be mature about it," Dad said. "Luc chose to live his life at other people's expense. He chose to enjoy his drinks and do absolutely nothing useful."

I felt shocked. I felt horrible. I felt like I did something really, really terrible. Uncle Luc never returned the money. My mother tried to comfort me by saying that kindness is how the world heals, whatever that means. Together with Grandma, Mom gave me another $25 to buy the rock collection, but every time I played with it, I couldn't help thinking about Uncle Luc and my father. Later, I started carrying one of those rocks in my pocket to remind myself that I have to be reasonable. If I really think about it, some people do not deserve help. Only people who work hard deserve things. I will grow up to be one of those smart, hard-working, deserving people.

I know the motto Jack and I share is slightly different from this personal one. I know that Jack's interpretation of being reasonable is more far-reaching. But is it really

that different? I learned not to help people like Uncle Luc.
Jack learned not to help the homeless. Or a kid with intel-
lectual limitations who's wrongfully convicted of murder.
They are not deserving.

I'm no different from Jack.

And what does a person deserve anyway?

Do I really deserve all that I have and all that I can do?
And does anyone who is in deep trouble deserve what
they get? Or, are they just unlucky?

I get the rock out of my pocket, breathe in deeply and
throw it as far into the water as I can. My solid life motto
goes underwater with a splash.

43

Chapter 7

Two more weeks means two more rounds until the end of the experiment. I start the next round feeling like I'm on autopilot. I think about changing the sliders under the "veil of ignorance" to improve the rules and regulations of *Just City*, but I feel overwhelmed. I thought the U.S. laws and regulations were fair, that's why I left the settings mostly at default positions previously. But now I feel like everything needs to be changed.

Clicking through the defaults, I slow down at the penal system section.

One option, in particular, catches my eye: allocation of additional government funding to programs such as the Innocence Project and something called "TRUE"—a program for young offenders. Most descriptions have virtual links to additional information. I click on the TRUE info and watch a short video about the program. The educational and rehabilitation focus makes incarceration for the program participants look more like a summer camp. I can't help being impressed by one of the life-timer mentors (yes, a prisoner himself!) of the TRUE program participants. His reason for mentoring is redemption. He doesn't want his life to be a waste.

Is this stuff real? These are real websites, and I can't imagine my grandma's team would create all this for the game if it didn't exist in real life. But I have to move on. I slightly adjust the slider to allow for such programs in *Just City*, even though it's not like I'm going to prison again in this round. My character in the last round would have definitely benefited from this, but I understand that in this round, my character may get into a totally different type of trouble. It's like everything will have to be changed if I think this way. With sadness, I remember how excited I was to play the first round of *Just City*. Now I feel hopeless and choose just to leave all the other settings as they are.

The new round starts. The veil of ignorance is lifted. The loser life of an emigrant worker only brings me an additional 350 points.

And silence from the gang.

They haven't suggested meeting since my fight with Jack. Did he tell them about the fight? That wouldn't surprise me now.

Tomorrow I'm planning to video chat with my parents. The last time we spoke, I told them how great things were going, all excited about our startup. Dad's annoying comments about how it's not that easy to have a successful startup didn't even spoil the tone of the conversation. His super-successful son was on the way to his next success.

Right...

I don't even know what is supposed to be happening now. What does this all mean? Are Jack and I still going to apply? Are we even going to talk to each other again? I'm obviously not going to get enough money for the application. So, what am I supposed to do about that?

Dreading the chat with my parents and needing some clarity, I decide to text Jack."What's up?" I type much slower than usual.

"Nothing much," he texts back. "Sent off the paperwork for my startup."

"You... what?" I type but then delete without sending. I reread his last message several times.

I can't believe it. I sit down on the bed and stare at the floor. It means I'm out. He went in without me. I should have expected it, after all that's happened, but I guess I still hoped it was fixable... My throat feels dry and contracted.

I could try going for the startup competition by myself. I could come up with a different startup idea and do it without Jack, but the money I will get for the game is nowhere near what I need and... it wasn't supposed to be like this. I bow and hold my heavy head in my hands.

Chapter 8

I t's a gloomy Monday. The last week of the game has begun. I haven't been doing much in the last two weeks: playing the game for about two hours daily, surfing online, and binge-watching shows for hours.

The music, the dice roll, the sliders... I don't care. The veil of ignorance lifts, and things suddenly look different. Everything becomes black and white. I see my dirty hands first, with scratches and bruises. I'm a homeless man who suffers from Major Depressive Disorder. Everywhere I go in the game, people turn away from me. I wonder which of them are preprogrammed characters and who are test players. And everything is freaking black and white. Obviously, accomplishing "life tasks" —finding a job in *Just City*, establishing relationships with other players, and virtually engaging in leisure activities and hobbies—doesn't go smoothly.

But it feels right because it is how I've been feeling recently.

My character has encounters with the police, gets sick because of malnutrition, takes drugs, and gets beaten up by some punks. There is no help in sight.

On Wednesday, my character's actions are again hijacked by the game, as happened during my second round. He pushes his shopping cart along the streets and stops near a huge multistory housing project (where I get my drugs sometimes—I mean, he does). The algorithm forces me to walk into the building, take the elevator to the top floor, go to the roof, and jump.

It's only Wednesday; the game round technically continues till Monday, but all I see now on the screen is a view from above: my dead body next to the shopping cart. The total number of points averaged over the four rounds, with penalties, is an astonishingly low number. Sixty-three.

Chapter 9

On Monday, I fill out some questionnaires, get my $563 for the study, and tell Grandma everything I thought about her game. This money is definitely not enough for me to go for the startup competition by myself. My numerous applications for paid summer internships remain unanswered. And what would the startup be about anyway?

This week has been gloomy, and I haven't felt like going for runs. This morning I realized it has been two weeks since Jack and I texted, and he told me he was going for the competition by himself. I am still mad at Jack. A couple of times, I imagine how he actually composed and typed up the anonymous complaint letter back at the Geniuses Club and then met with me and hung out like nothing happened. Has he always been playing me? I thought he really cared about me. I thought being cool, somewhat reserved, and distant was just his style. Has he ever opened up?

There was one moment, back in the days of the Geniuses Club, when he came to our gathering with a pale face. He looked sad. During the break, I asked him what was going on, and he said his childhood chess teacher, Petro, had died. I remember how I paused and decided not to try to cheer him up right away. Instead, I said I was sorry and stayed quiet waiting for him to share, and it actually worked. Jack told me Petro was probably more important to him than his father. Back in Jack's "fat bullied kid" days, Petro always treated him with respect. He told Jack that he had to choose what to do about his situation. So, Jack did. That's when he turned his life around.

That's the only time I remember Jack opening up with me even a tiny bit. Instead of making me feel better and less mad, this memory makes me feel worse. I feel... loss. But why? Because I miss our fake friendship?

In the afternoon, just like the day before, I start to feel a weird pain. Chest? Stomach? I can't locate it, but I really want it to stop. Should I go to a doctor? I don't even know what I'm complaining about. They will ask, "What are your complaints?" What would I say? "Pain of a non-existing organ of the body."

Having dinner at Grandma's every Thursday has been our tradition for a long time. Today is Thursday. I force myself to get up and go across the street. Secretly I hope she can tell me what I should do. I feel like I'm in a hole; my understanding of the world is shattered, my friendship with Jack is shattered, and my dream about a startup is shattered.

During dinner, Grandma hesitantly asks me, "So you haven't met with your friends recently?" I previously told her a very brief version of what had happened.

"No," I reply, thinking maybe I can share more with her.

"Have you talked to your parents about it?" she asks.

"No," I frown. "Grandma, don't tell them anything, ok?" I know she is unlikely to tell them anything, but still... I am really not ready for them to know what a loser I am, especially my dad. I know they are in the search-and-hire process for a new employee for their hydroponic farm. The last time we talked, Dad told me he would rather have me in that position over the summer, and maybe permanently once I'm done with college. It just again proves that Dad doesn't even imagine the possibility of me becoming an entrepreneur on my own.

"Of course not, Nathan. I won't tell them," Grandma replies, and I believe her. Grandma has always been on my side. When I was going to start college in the city, my parents were worried about whether it was safe for me to live here by myself. Grandma gave them the crime statistics regarding the part of the city where she lived and said that if I rented an apartment there, the risk would be minimal, and she would be close in case I wanted to come over for dinner. I was grateful because that convinced my parents and gave me freedom. I also love that Grandma is never opinionated and always neutral. She never tells me how to live my life, and in a way, she is a perfect sounding board. But there has always been a distance between us, maybe because she is so neutral.

I decide not to share more and not to ask her what to do. Grandma looks at me sympathetically as we quietly finish dinner. I realize that I'm sitting hunched, one arm around my abdomen—what a pathetic picture.

When I come home, I feel even worse than before. I need to do something that will lift me up. I remembered my plan to ask Jocelyn out. This doesn't seem like a realistic option at all. I haven't talked to the gang since the game. Jack and I are like a divorced couple, in which he got all the friends.

Can music lift my mood? Not the type I usually like listening to. Suddenly the buoyant Twenty-something song from the *Just City* game intro plays in my head, and I decide to Google it to cheer myself up. It sounds so upbeat and carefree. I want to reach that state again. I start watching the music video for the song. The black-and-white video tells a story of a young Latino man who gets out of jail in San Diego, determined to turn his life around for the sake of his family. But it looks like the system presents him with obstacles at every turn, such as potential employers tearing his resume into pieces and throwing it into a trash can the moment he leaves the room, forcing him back into a life of crime to take care of his family. This leads to him being arrested and taken away in a police car in front of his wife and two little children.

I burst into tears, something that hasn't happened since I was a child. I feel so saddened, even heartbroken, by this unexpected video, but again, this totally makes sense for the *Just City* game's intro song. It might as well be another scenario in the game. It probably is. But the worst part is that it's probably somebody's real life.

I go to bed early. I feel pain for myself, the Latino guy from the music video, and everyone else whose life is a mess. Dreams of not existing feel almost pleasant.

Chapter 10

The following morning, I lie on my bed for hours after waking up. My clothes are scattered on the floor, and I just keep staring at the wall. I've never behaved like this in my life. How can someone just lie there all day, in a mess? I never understood such people. This reminds me of Monica's mom.

When I was 16, I realized I really liked my classmate Monica—always sweet, modestly dressed, and often smiling. There was this warmth about her. I was considering asking her on a date. One day I got a chance to walk her home. We were working on a project together, and she needed help bringing a bunch of beakers to her place. On the way there, a stray puppy started following us, and without much hesitation, she said she would take the puppy home.

"Are you sure?" I asked. "Will your mom be okay with it?"

Monica smiled and said, "It wouldn't be the first time."

I kept asking what her mother would say. Monica said her mother didn't say much in general, so it was okay. I wasn't sure I understood her. When we came to her place and she opened the door, I noticed how beat down the apartment was. Torn wallpaper with traces of water leaks, old boxes and rugs everywhere, and visible sand and dirt on the floor—nothing like the clean and cozy place I grew up in. However, the most shocking thing was three other dogs running toward Monica. I could see Monica's mother lying on a couch in the living room. We said hello to each other from a distance, but she didn't come to greet us.

On my way home, I thought about Monica, her mother, their dogs, and their life. Why did they choose to live like that? I was still attracted to and fascinated by Monica, but it also scared me because I didn't understand how someone could live like that. It seemed like they didn't think about the consequences. It seemed very unreasonable. I decided not to ask Monica out because of what I saw and because it appeared to me that her compassion, which I liked, came at the price of being very messed up.

Now I'm lying here in bed, just like Monica's mom, not doing anything, not being able to do anything. It was so natural for me to judge her in my head. It doesn't feel as natural anymore.

In the evening, I decide to call my mom. When I video chat with both of my parents every couple of weeks, I usually update them on how things are going in terms of recent events and achievements. We don't discuss feelings much. But this time, I call her directly and ask her about what I was like when I was a little child. She tells me about many nice little things, such as how I liked it when she read to me. Then she says, "There was this picture book called..." and we finish the sentence simultaneously, "Corduroy." We laugh. It was a sweet story about a stuffed toy bear who came to life. He lost a button, and no one wanted to take him home because of this imperfection. I remember it so vividly. I think those were the best moments in my life, hearing, again and again, my mom read to me how a little girl helps the bear and takes him home. The joy of seeing someone in need being helped was profound. I wished all defective, lonely toys could be found, helped, and cared for. I thought I would have done the same as that girl. My biggest inner wish was to help those who were lonely. Somewhere along the way, that desire was suppressed by the thought that not everyone deserves help. But the memories of the joy from reading that book always stayed with me.

The conversation with Mom does make me feel a bit better. Despite wanting to give up on everything recently, I think maybe I can still try. Still try to have a startup... Maybe something will still come out of me.

Maybe I will even clean up my apartment. What a mess.

Chapter 11

Today, I finally clean my apartment. As I eat dinner, I play around with the thought of going for the startup competition on my own. Just hypothetically. What would my idea be?

I search through the notes that I took on my phone during the startup meetings and find a list titled How to Come Up with a Startup Idea:

- Identify pain points / Solve a problem

- Copy what works

- Use your skillset

- Get a change of scenery

- Meditate

I remember how Jack and I looked at each other and chuckled when the guest CEO said, "Meditate." So new-agey... Jack's idea to track shopping carts came directly from identifying pain points and solving a problem.

I look at the list now, and "Copy what works" makes me ponder. I need to know what the jury will be looking for.

I go for a walk. It's chilly, and the streets are relatively empty. I pass several construction sites surrounding the convention center plaza. The center brings many visitors when a convention takes place but not today. I cross the drawbridge and head to the Green Gym that is supposed to have a grand opening sometime soon. Green Gym is one of the New Entrepreneur Incubator's recent startups. It's an interesting idea of a gym, which will be electrically powered by the members' cycling, lifting, and other types of workouts. Can I come up with a cool idea like that?

I'm walking past an old homeless man sitting on the sidewalk begging for money. My first automatic thought: *He stinks, and I want to avoid walking too close*. Then a second thought pops up: *He is having a really bad "round."* The imaginary dice roll... The *Just City* game has messed with my head. I think about how lucky I am to have a place to live in. I give the homeless man $10, not worrying anymore about how it would "spoil him" and not worrying about what Jack would say.

I cross the railroad tracks and arrive at the Green Gym. I explore the peculiar building from the outside because the grand opening is not until next Friday. Air plants hang along the walls, making it look green. After some time, I decide to walk back home, as it's getting dark. I pass the railroad, thinking about whether Green Gym will have to supplement the electric power with other sources besides bicycles and other equipment. Did they have any solar panels on the roof?

Still immersed in my thoughts, I suddenly feel a strong, sharp pain in my left knee. Something hit me. I jump back and see the old homeless man sitting at the sidewalk's edge, holding a metal pipe. A metal pipe he has just hit me with!

I bend forward and grab my knee with both hands to reduce the pain. For a moment, I'm just trying to assess the situation. I don't really see his facial expression because it's quite dark. He is just sitting there with the pipe, holding it limply, and probably not going to attack again. He doesn't say anything, and neither do I. Still shocked and frightened, I back away farther and make a big loop to get to the creek bridge without getting anywhere close to him.

My knee is still hurting, and I'm angry and confused. It's so unfair! I gave him money, and this is the thanks I get. The wind is getting stronger, so typical for summer in the city. As I reach the bridge, I slow down and stop to process for a moment what happened. I'm standing on the bridge, looking at the water, hiding my neck in my jacket. I keep thinking about the homeless man, and as my anger subsides, different thoughts come and start repeating themselves. *He is having a bad "round..."* as if we were in the *Just City* game. Except that we are now talking about real life. Still, the "bad round" explanation doesn't sit well with me because it's so crazy! I would never do something like this! Okay, he had a different economic situation, but to be like that, I mean, to hit someone who just gave you 10 bucks with a metal pipe, out of the blue—how would I ever be able to do that? I start hearing in my head Grandma's words about the brain and how I would have done the same (whatever "same" means—confessing to a crime I didn't commit or hitting someone with a pipe) if everything were the same: the genes and every bit of the environment, all the events... It could have been me. Unbelievable, but it could have been me. Hitting someone with a metal pipe out of the blue, probably due to some mental health issues, which are also in the brain's structure and function... It could have been me.

I suddenly hear someone saying laughingly, "L-o-s-e-r!" A young couple smelling like weed is passing by. Obviously, the comment is about me; no one else is around. I guess standing on a bridge staring at the water, all hunched and in what is the opposite of a power pose, looks really pathetic. For some reason, this comment doesn't upset me. I find it kind of funny... It's also funny, or ironic, how my whole understanding of life is now upside down because of some has-nothing-to-do-with-real-life philosophy experiment.

I come home and check my emails. One of the emails announces that I am invited to interview for an internship that will start next week—the only one out of all that I applied for. It's a software engineering internship, it would pay ridiculously well, and I may be able to have $10K by September 1. Incredible.

Chapter 12

It's Tuesday, July 6. After a short interview, which seemed like a formality, I'm starting my internship. It will hopefully be my ticket to the startup competition. The money I'll get for the summer is less than $10K. Still, if I do well, they may offer me part-time work during the school year and, thanks to one of the trending HR perks, pay the advance on September 1—perfect timing for me to get the full pre-seed funding for the startup competition.

It's mostly coding, and I know I'm great at that.

Today I'm working through the onboarding process and meeting with Alex, the supervising data scientist in the company. Alex is a young, Eastern-European-looking man who is very warm and welcoming.

As Alex and I have a late-afternoon chat in an open-space office, a cleaning lady comes by and empties the trash cans.

"Julissa, so nice to see you. How is your son doing?" Alex asks with genuine interest.

"Much better, Alex, thank you. Finally sleeping through the night."

The cleaning lady has gray hair and a limp. I don't usually pay much attention to people who do this kind of work.

The three of us have a brief chat about my internship. In the process, Alex helps Julissa move some recyclable materials from the trash can, which were put there mistakenly.

After Julissa leaves, I tell Alex, "That's nice of you, the way you talk with Julissa." I think about how Dad always keeps a polite distance from people not at his social level.

Alex smiles and says, "Be kind whenever possible. It is always possible. Dalai Lama."

Wow, that's a cool approach, and there is not a hint of arrogance in how Alex says it. None of my friends would quote something like that. I always thought of my friends as nice people. Or at least not "not nice." But now I'm unsure. This is like a whole other level.

———— ◆ ————

Over the past two weeks, Alex and I have been chatting more often, and we usually have lunch together. Alex and his sister Maria sometimes hang out in a café across the street after work. Last Friday, they invited me to join them for the first time, and we have met twice after work this week. It's been fun, and maybe also, on some level, I want to have a great relationship with Alex since he'll be the one to decide about the extension of my internship.

Maria has a baby, Lucy, a tiny, sweet girl she usually brings to the café.

Today we are in the café again. Maria is showing Alex some brochures for immigrants. Maria and Alex immigrated from Eastern Europe about three years ago when they were in their late twenties.

"Alex, what do you think this means? Did you have to do this?"

As Alex reads, I ask Maria, "Are you still in the bureaucratic process?"

"Luckily, I'm done myself, but I volunteer with my friend Lora to help other immigrants with translations and paperwork. Sometimes I can't understand how to translate, though." Maria smiles.

"That's so nice of you," I say. Even though Maria is a single mom taking care of her baby, she still finds time to volunteer and do this work. This is so different from other people. Do I mean, "different from Jack?" They care about other people, the environment, and things like that. But not in a preachy way at all.

Lucy starts to cry a little, and Maria takes her out of the stroller and starts rocking her. I look at this little creature, thinking for some reason about free will, brain development, and all that stuff that Grandma talks about. Maria catches my prolonged look and asks, "Would you like to hold her?"

I feel scared for a moment. I'm an only child and have never held a baby, but I want to impress Maria and Alex, and so I extend my hands. The baby feels lighter than I thought. Lucy kicks her tiny toes and makes a gurgling sound like she's happy in my arms. I feel proud of my unexpected success.

Maria looks delighted. "Children and animals sense a good person. You can't fool them. You are much better with her than some of the nannies at the daycare."

It feels so good to hear that. I've never held a baby in my life, and I'm better than the nannies at the daycare. Does Lucy feel something good in me? Trying not to reveal this thought process, I ask, "You use a daycare?"

"Sometimes," Maria replies. "When I go to the meditation center, Lucy stays there for an hour or two. The nannies are okay, but they pressure me because I refuse to give Lucy those dangerous vaccines. They have no right to do that."

"Oh." I feel sorry for Maria. That sounds bad. I was always vaccinated because my parents decided I should be, but can a daycare force it on someone?

"You should come with us to the meditation center," Alex jumps into our conversation with an enthusiastic tone. "Tomorrow is Tuesday, which is when we usually go."

"Sure," I reply automatically. Meditation has always sounded a little boring and unproductive to me. Jack would say it's totally new-agey, but it can't hurt to go once since Alex wants me to. Besides, it was on the list of ways to develop a startup idea. Unless it's some kind of a cult.

Chapter 13

After work, Alex and I meet up with Maria, and we walk 10 blocks to the small, pink building of the meditation center. We go through the little lobby into a beautiful meditation room lit by the setting sun, then sit down on colorful cushions on the floor. I side-eye Alex and Maria to see how seriously they are taking all this in order to gauge my reactions. They seem to be quite relaxed. *Probably not a cult,* I say to myself. The instructor, a middle-aged white man, briefly greets us and starts talking in a deep and calm voice.

"As you take a deep breath in and out, let all your worries be exhaled. You can close your eyes and relax your shoulders. Now imagine that your temporary body starts expanding, filled with light, expanding beyond this room, this district, this city, this country. Encompassing everything around."

I decide I want to do it right and follow the instructions. Maybe it will impress Alex, who knows? I imagine my body, the outer boundary of the skin, expanding. In my imagination, the skin soon starts to resemble a thin film, like a soap bubble. The inside of it—all that used to be my body—becomes shimmering light. The imagined expansion feels like a release of some tight restraint. My breathing changes, and my chest rises and falls in rhythm with the instructor's voice. I start feeling light and carefree and really happy. It may sound ridiculous, but I'm not sure I have ever felt this happy.

"There is no distinction between you and the world. There is only light and kindness. Spend the next 10 minutes not thinking about abstract concepts––and all words are abstract concepts––just be here, breathe and be here."

I breathe in deeply and slowly release the air through my nostrils, feeling so peaceful. I'm not sure if I have ever noticed how I breathe before or that I breathe at all, for that matter.

The instructor keeps talking, and I completely lose track of time.

"And as you return to yourself, your human self, think about the principles that govern your life, find the wisdom in yourself and become the principles you follow in everyday life."

I hear this part about life principles, which sounds interesting, but I feel so good that there are no coherent thoughts in my head.

The meditation ends, and people start to slowly get up from their cushions, but I don't want to move or go anywhere.

Wow, that was something. I don't want to tell Alex and Maria how much I liked this meditation session because, a) I don't feel like talking at all, and b) I don't want to tell them that I'm a grownup in his twenties who is just now discovering how easily he can change his mental state. I wonder about all the things meditation could have helped me with, like giving presentations and being super nervous. Can I use it in the future for my startup ideas?

Luckily, Alex and Maria don't ask me about my experience and just say I'm welcome to join them anytime they come here. On my way home, I try to remember what exactly the instructor was saying, wondering why the meditation had such an effect on me. I can't remember much or anything special, but I do remember that at the end, he asked about the principles governing my life.

I used to have a life motto based on reason and working hard, which would make me "deserving." I miss that feeling of confidence. My life motto, life credo, has died, drowned, together with that rock I threw into the bay after playing *Just City*.

What does one do after a life credo dies? Do you just come up with a different one? I think about Alex's words about being kind. That it's always possible. Alex always seems to be following it in his life. It makes me think of my mom, too; she is similar in that way, although she never shares much about her views. Grandma too; she is very kind. If I were to come up with new principles that govern my life, I guess kindness would somehow be involved. At least it would be nice.

Chapter 14

Next Thursday, during dinner at my grandma's, I tell her about Alex and Maria and going to meditation with them. As I speak, I realize how excited I am about these things.

"You know, Grandma, they are so different from my other friends. They are so kind and spiritual."

Grandma suddenly looks up and almost spills the water for the tea. She always listens attentively to me but now appears even more alert. I continue to tell her about my amazing experience at the meditation center.

"Oh, a meditation center... nice." Grandma speaks slowly and to my surprise, looks reserved rather than excited.

The way she says "nice" sounds formal and insincere. Even her posture looks stiff. I feel like she is not happy for me, and I don't understand why. It makes me feel nervous.

"I'm doing much better," I continue. "Aren't you happy for me? What is it—don't you meditate yourself?"

"Of course, I'm happy. And yes, I do practice meditation myself."

"But?" I still feel like something is going on.

"The last thing I want is to impose my views on you. I just want you..." she pauses, "To think for yourself. Sorry, I am happy that you are feeling better."

"Think for myself?" I can't ignore her weird reaction. "What are you talking about? Is there something dangerous about being spiritual? They are really nice, kind people. It's not a cult," I add, still puzzled by what caused her reaction.

"I know," she says. Then she mumbles quietly, "It just reminds me of..." She shakes her head and doesn't finish the sentence. A little hurt by her reaction, I don't ask more.

So much for Grandma being kind.

At home later, I think again about how Grandma was suddenly so judgmental. She has never been that way with me before. And what was it about this that reminds her of something? I thought Grandma cared about me so much that she would always be on my side. Maybe the whole being-really-kind thing is not that prevalent in my family. But my mom is different, although I feel like Mom's kind nature is often hidden behind her always agreeing with Dad. I imagine how wonderful it would be to grow up in a family where everyone is really, really kind, like my new friends. We would eat dinner together and discuss things we could do for others, not just ourselves and our achievements. And lending someone money, even if they are an alcoholic, could be considered a good thing.

Chapter 15

The next evening, I hang out with Alex, Maria, and little Lucy in the café again. I look at them and remember Grandma's strange behavior from the previous evening. Right now, I feel closer to them than to her. I wonder if my real values—whatever they are—may be closer to their values than my family's.

Maria is telling Alex about their friend who was supposed to be Lucy's godfather but suddenly had to leave the country because of legal issues. It's not even clear when or if he will come back.

"I don't know what to do. I hoped to have the ceremony this Sunday. I know it's against the tradition to have a relative, but maybe you could do it?" Maria asks Alex, concerned. "I know the whole thing is a formality, and I'm doing it more for our mom. Knowing how religious she became before her death, I'm sure she would have insisted."

I think about Maria, who volunteers to help immigrants, and have this spontaneous urge to save the day. "Can anyone be the godfather? I would be happy to."

Maria is speechless for a second, but then she smiles so warmly. "Nathan, that would be amazing! You are such a kind soul."

"Will the authorities allow it? What exactly do I have to do?" I ask and, at the same time, sense how my feeling of enthusiasm overpowers any of my concerns.

"You don't have to have any specific affiliation, and it's a very simple ceremony, actually done at home. There aren't any specific things you have to do after the ceremony, just generally take an interest in your godchild."

I feel really good about this. I know Alex and Maria don't have many friends here in the U.S.

The ceremony takes place the following Sunday at Maria's apartment. I feel excited, and curious to see what it may look like. I bring a little gift for Lucy, a book titled "Physics for Babies."

When I arrive, only Alex, Maria, and Lucy are there. We are waiting for the godmother and the priest. I look around as we wait. I like the space, especially the thin rugs with geometric patterns hanging on the walls.

I almost feel like a family member participating in a family gathering, like a birthday. The doorbell rings and Maria jokes, "Your other half for today has arrived." Lucy's godmother is Maria's friend and neighbor, Lora. I've heard them talk about her, but we never met. She walks in, stunningly beautiful and with the kindest smile. After we are introduced, she says, "I've heard the nicest things about you, Nathan," and hugs me. I wonder what they told her about me and find it incredible how one can form such close friendships with a new group of people in such a short time. I feel lucky. And a little bit mesmerized by Lora.

The priest comes to Maria's apartment a little late. He performs a short ceremony by saying prayers and splashing some water on Lucy.

During the ceremony, Lora's head is covered with a dark green scarf, from under which flow waves of her beautiful red hair. Lucy cries for the second half of the ceremony, but it's soon over.

I keep glancing at Lora and smiling.

We all leave soon after the ceremony. Lucy needs to nap, and we don't want to disturb her sleep. I barely get a chance to talk to Lora. I only learn that she is 23, a photographer, and lives in a house nearby. I also learn that I will likely think about her a lot.

Chapter 16

It's Tuesday evening. I'm sitting on a bench outside the meditation center, under a bush full of bright purple flowers. I'm waiting for Alex, Maria, and Lora to arrive. Okay, I'm waiting for Lora. Yesterday, when Alex asked if I was coming, I said, "Sure. Will Lora come too?"

Alex smiled and said, "I can ask her."

Here they are. Here they all are. While Alex and Maria, after waving at me, keep heading toward the entrance, Lora approaches and sits on the bench next to me.

"Nathan, how nice to see you. How are you? How was your day?" She looks into my eyes with such startling presence, meaning what she is saying.

"It was a fun day of code optimization. I am proud of my negative progress," I reply.

"Negative progress?" she asks, looking confused.

"On some days, I am productive and write like a hundred lines of code. Today I shortened my code by about a hundred lines. It's a good thing." I smile. "How about you?"

Lora laughs. "I traveled a hundred miles to take photos of a client who turned out not to be there."

"Really?"

"Well, I had a suspicion when talking to her on the phone that she might not be super reliable about scheduled appointments. There has been a lot of back and forth about today's appointment. A lot."

"Was it a mistake to take on such a client?" I ask.

"I don't think there is such a thing as a mistake."

"There isn't?" I lean a notch closer to Lora. I can catch a faint flowery smell coming from her hair. I love how much her green eyes shine. I feel so light inside.

"Every event in life is a gift if only you can see it. If you trust life, it starts working with you, not against you. All the universe conspires to help you achieve your dreams. What you send out with your thoughts, with a loving intention, will come to you, and sometimes in surprising ways."

"Really?" Wow, it feels so good to listen to her words.

"When I was returning home from my client's town today, I met this amazing woman on the train who will be perfect for my portrait project." Lora opens her eyes wide with joy. "Synchronicity."

"Synchronicity," I repeat, enchanted.

I know it's time to go because the meditation is starting soon, but I wish we could stay here on the bench. Lora and I have been talking for 10 minutes, but I feel like we've known each other for an eternity.

As we join Alex and Maria in the tiny lobby of the center, Lora quietly asks me, "So it's not your first time here, right? What brought you here?"

"I'm here for the cookies." I make a serious face and point at the tea corner.

Lora laughs, looks at Maria and Alex, and says, "We've been coming here for two years now, right?"

"And why are you here?" I ask.

"It's all about love," says Alex. "Replacing the dogmas of this sometimes heartless world with love—that's what can help all of us heal."

"Oh, Alex, that's too deep. I like the cookie reply much better." Lora keeps giggling.

I think about what Alex means by "dogmas." And the word "love" surprises me... It does seem to be quite profound.

The meditation this time is slightly less deep for me, as my thoughts keep turning to Lora, sitting not far from me. But the instructor's words at the end about "the principles that govern my everyday life" catch my attention again. The term "love" from the previous conversation pops up in my head again. All of them—Alex, Maria, and Lora—have, in one way or another, mentioned something like this. The way they use the word "love" is unusual to me. I feel a tiny bit uncomfortable but also attracted by the idea of focusing on the notion of love so much when thinking about one's life. It's similar to kindness but even deeper, more all-encompassing. I feel the warmth inside and open my eyes. I can't help but turn my head and look at Lora. Her beautiful face with closed eyes looks angelic.

Chapter 17

Today for meditation, it's only Lora and me. Alex and Maria are meeting with the immigrants they are helping. I wonder if it's a good opportunity to ask Lora to dinner after the meditation—something I've probably wanted since I met her at Maria's that first time. It would be a test of whether she likes me. It's one thing to hang out among friends; it's another thing to go on an actual date.

The session is a little different today: compassion meditation. We are invited to feel one with the world. To dissolve the sense of ego. After the introductory meditation, I feel a warmth inside my chest.

I keep my eyes closed as the facilitator says, "There is a simple approach to dissolving the feeling of anger against others, dissolving the feeling of separation between yourself and others. Think this: *Everyone is me in disguise...* Everyone is you..."

The facilitator's voice continues, "Through the power of deep listening... listening with my heart and with my mind and with my soul, I connect with other people, knowing that the other is myself, just in disguise. And by connecting to the other, I will let go of my ego, of my separate self. And by connecting to the other, I will connect with the whole universe."

It's so strange; his words remind me of *Just City*. "Sooner or later, you play all the roles." This guided meditation and *Just City*'s idea of a random assignment of who you are—there are clear parallels between these two things, although they are presented in such different settings. Grandma presented this idea in the game from her scientific perspective. Maybe science and spiritual traditions are saying the same thing, just in different ways. I'm still grappling with understanding why Grandma was so unsupportive of me meditating.

After the session, I ask Lora if she wants to have dinner together, and to my relief, she says yes. She suggests going to a vegan restaurant, Golden Era, which I can live with. I prefer something with meat, but going on a date with Lora and making a good impression matters more to me, and it works. Our conversation flows, and I can't get enough of looking at her across the table. After we eat, I walk Lora home. I wish I could hang out with her longer, but tomorrow morning I have to help Alex with a presentation at work.

"Is Alex a strict boss?" Lora asks.

"You have no idea." I laugh because we both know how non-strict he is. We decide I'll come in just for half an hour.

Lora is renting the ground floor of a family house. It's an extended studio, with the landlords living upstairs. It's modest but beautiful inside. There is a bed, a couch, and a table that she uses both as a desk and kitchen table. A shelf with photography supplies sits in a corner. Something catches my eye near the window: a small table, like a mini altar, with flowers and many cute little objects: a photo of her parents in a frame, several candles, precious rocks, dried herbs in bunches, and little bottles with labels reading, "homeopathic path."

We drink tea, and Lora offers to do a tarot card reading for me. She asks me to think of something weighing on my mind, something I want to get clarity about. She says not to tell her what it is. I think about my startup. What should it be about? And will it be successful? Lora gets a deck of beautifully decorated cards and asks me to slowly pull three cards. She puts them on the table and turns the first one. The card depicts an ugly man laughing.

"This card represents the past related to what you are thinking about. What I see here is betrayal."

I almost choke on my tea. She turns the second card and says that it represents the present.

"A scale with golden chalices—you are undecided and may run out of time."

"I assume the last card is the future?" I ask, finding the whole thing freakish but also eager to see what it is. Oh, I hope it's something good.

She turns the last card. "The path of the heart will bring you resolution."

"The path of the heart?" I keep staring at the card. "Any step-by-step instructions?" It would be great to get specifics on what I should do about my startup. Does the path of the heart mean it should be about something I really like?

Lora talks a little bit about following one's heart in general—how one gets to one's heart's truth only after peeling off everyone else's opinions and expectations. Of course, she doesn't even know what topic I have in mind. I'm so glad she is not asking because I would then have to talk about the business with Jack, and I don't feel like doing that right now.

I feel like spending more time with Lora, but I soon leave. Before I go, she hugs me and kisses me good night on the cheek. I feel pleased by how our first date went but also puzzled by the card reading.

At home, I can't fall asleep. I think about Lora, feeling warmth and excitement. I think about her tarot card reading. I sit on my bed and decide to do the compassion meditation exercise given to us as homework at the meditation center. First, I try to feel compassion for someone I love. I think about Mom. It's so easy for me to feel love and compassion for her. I remember our book readings when I was a child. My mom, in her hand-knit purple sweater, sitting by my bed, reading to me passionately every night no matter what, as if it were the most important thing in her day. My chest feels warm and soft. Then, I try to feel compassion for myself, sending good wishes to myself the way our instructor taught us. *May I be happy. May I be well. May I be peaceful and at ease.*

Am I really feeling compassion for myself? It feels more challenging. Dad probably would say this exercise does not help build a strong character. Working hard does. But I think of myself during those times when Mom used to read to me. I was just a child. My brain was still forming. All the influences on that brain were taking place, as my grandma would put it. This approach kind of works, and I feel compassion for my child self. Then I'm supposed to pick someone more challenging. I think about Jack. The tarot card with the ugly man laughing pops up in my memory. For a moment, the feeling of resentment starts to approach my throat, making it contract. I still feel angry about his betrayal back in the Geniuses Club and him talking behind my back in the *Just City* game. I make myself think about the meditation teacher's words, *Everyone is me in disguise*. Or Grandma's version, *It could have been me*. Actually, with Jack, this thought is really easy. I have always felt close to him in many ways, and I did share his opinions, like playing smart and getting ahead. And when I did share those opinions, that was me, not somebody else.

I suddenly start thinking about rejecting that blind guy applying to the Geniuses Club. It seemed like a rational decision. How about Jack making himself the president of the club by removing me? Well, he probably had his rational reasons too. I suddenly remember that brief moment during our fight where I confronted Jack about the anonymous letter. Right after I confronted him, he paused and said, "Look, I never meant..." But I never let him finish. What was he going to say?

Maybe I'm not angry at Jack. Maybe it is me I have been angry with, about all my mistakes. I feel heaviness in my chest, and my throat feels coarse and dry.

Suddenly a tear starts running down my cheek. I feel so sad and... not ashamed, but... what am I feeling? Remorse. I feel remorse about going cold rational on people, intentionally separating myself from their troubles, and not being kind. My mom has always been right. Kindness is the most important thing. Or, using my new vocabulary, *It's all about love*.

I wish I had been kind all my life. Instead, I think that sometimes I was... horrible. Remorse is definitely what I'm feeling. Strangely, this feeling of remorse feels like a relief. Maybe it's that self-compassion kicking in, I don't know. Maybe it's Lora, her positivity, and her "mistakes don't exist" point of view... I wonder what I can do differently. How can one live... kindness, love, compassion? It's not like I can make it my job. Even though I don't dislike the idea of charities like I used to, it's not like I would ever make my career in it. I still want to be an entrepreneur. I still want to create a cool startup!

I should go to sleep now.

Chapter 18

The next evening I'm at my grandma's, and we are about to have dinner. There has been tension between us since that conversation two weeks ago, when she suddenly got all judgmental about Alex, Maria, and the meditation center. I still don't understand what came over her. She has never been like that with me before. I hope we can get back to where our relationship was. Maybe if I tell Grandma about Lora, that would help? She always listened with curiosity and openness to anything I had to say about my past girlfriends. I'm sure Grandma will be happy to hear I met someone I like so much.

After we finish our meal, I notice a flyer on her kitchen table from Golden Era. Wow, that's a perfect opportunity to talk about Lora. I casually say, "Lora is right; once you get more attuned to them, synchronicities are more likely to happen. I just ate at this restaurant yesterday."

Instead of asking who Lora is, Grandma suddenly frowns. Grandma never frowns. Man, what's going on? She says, dead serious, "Nathan, you know that people are excellent at pattern recognition, and at the same time, we have a very poor understanding of probabilities. We tend to notice coincidence when two events seem to have a connection with each other, and we see that coincidence as highly improbable."

I can see Grandma breathe in and out, her nostrils widen. She continues, "Because of this poor understanding of probabilities, some people think that there are no coincidences—that everything happens for a reason."

"Grandma, you know, Lora is my new girlfriend, a friend of Alex and Maria. She is amazing, and I like her." I still can't believe Grandma didn't even ask me who Lora was. "So, are you saying Lora has a poor understanding of probabilities? Or that I do?" I'm not enjoying this unexpected lecture.

"On an intuitive level, we all do." Grandma says, stressing the word "all." "Evolution led to this way in which humans think, and some people start seeing meaning in random things. It's one of the cognitive biases, the so-called 'meaning bias,' which is the need for the world to make sense or have some meaning. This naïve assessment ignores all the many events in our lives that do not line up. Add on top of that the 'confirmation bias,' the tendency to notice only what fits our already existing beliefs, and we are in trouble."

I don't like her using the word "naïve." I take it personally and frown, but she continues.

"Look, Nathan, this flyer..." She picks up the Golden Era flyer. "I don't mean to offend your new girlfriend, but it's even more important to tell you this because she is your girlfriend. We experience, hear, see, and dream thousands of things daily. By random chance alone, events should appear to line up occasionally. For example, you dream of a friend you haven't seen in 10 years, and they call the next day. In isolation, it seems amazing, but if there were never any such coincidences, that would be unusual and demand some explanation." Grandma takes out a tin can of green tea from the cupboard. I follow it with my eyes and, to avoid looking at Grandma, keep looking at the tin can as she continues.

"The belief in 'synchronistic' coincidences also neglects the fact that there are many people in the world. For example, in a city with one million people, a one-million-to-one coincidence should happen to someone every day! Such stories are likely to propagate because they are very compelling. Therefore, you're likely to hear stories of improbable coincidences. And this is just one from a whole pack of supernatural beliefs our minds evolved to be vulnerable to."

Grandma's words that a one-million-to-one coincidence should happen to someone every day in a city with one million people hit me with their obvious, mathematical truthfulness. But I'm disappointed that instead of asking me more about Lora and my feelings for her, Grandma criticizes my flyer comment. I can't help but resist. "Grandma, don't you think that as a scientist, you get a little close-minded sometimes?"

"I can't be happier to embrace new perspectives as long as the person presenting them brings me new evidence, collected and tested in an unbiased way." She pauses.

I don't buy it... I can't imagine finding enough evidence to change her mind about anything. Maybe some professor could do it... In silence, I keep thinking about whether I have any influence on Grandma. I also wonder why she's been like that —passionate, but not in a good way—whenever I tell her about my life recently. When I first told her about my friends and the meditation center, and she acted all weird for the first time, she said something about it reminding her of something or someone else. Maybe that's the thing, but I have no idea what exactly.

Suddenly Grandma says, "Don't tell me that your friends also don't immunize their children... or use homeopathy for serious conditions."

I immediately remember hearing Maria say that vaccines are dangerous. I also remember seeing several bottles of homeopathic medicine in Lora's apartment. I don't want to say that, so I go for a more general statement, trying to defend my friends with arguments I think they would use. "Many people say homeopathy helps them. Big pharma doesn't want you to use it, clearly."

"Nathan, homeopathy is a multi-billion dollar industry that doesn't need to spend money on research and development because there is no research and development! Meta-analyses convincingly show that it is no better than a placebo. That is not to say that there is no placebo effect—there definitely is—but it is to say that there is no physical mechanism for how homeopathy can work, and there should be no surprise it can't beat a placebo. You know that if I give the homeopathic 'medicine' to a chemist, they won't be able to detect a single molecule of the 'active ingredient' in it because of the dilution by a factor of one part in 10 power 30— power 30! Hahnemann, the 18th century inventor of homeopathy, believed such 'medicine' would still retain the chemical properties of what was being diluted—something that all of chemistry and biology says is impossible!"

I don't know what to say and leave for home early. I feel a bit resentful. Of course, Grandma knows so many things that I don't, but I simply wanted to tell her about Lora.

Even at home, I keep thinking about how Grandma talked to me. It's like she doesn't see me as an adult. I'm a grownup. I can choose what I do and think, and I can choose my friends, after all. I can live on my own and earn my living on my own. Does she doubt my startup dream too? She used to be behind it, and I felt like she always wanted to help me to be independent, but now I can easily imagine Grandma talking to my dad and saying, "Oh, maybe Nathan could work for your hydroponic farm?" I shiver at this image.

Here is what I will do. I will have my friends and girl-friend who are not afraid to believe what they believe. I will also come up with an awesome startup idea and the money for the startup all by myself. I will win the startup competition and be successful, surrounded by loving people. Grandma will see, and Dad will see. This idea of "being reasonable" that I got from Dad—what did it bring me? Selfish Jacks. I want loving people! I choose love and kindness over "being reasonable!"

I decide to find excuses and not have my weekly dinner with Grandma, at least for the next few weeks. I need to be with supportive people right now.

The following Thursday, Grandma's friend and former colleague Mark is coming for dinner, and I find it to be a perfect excuse, not wanting to disturb them. Although I always like hanging out with Mark because, despite being an academic, he knows a surprising number of anecdotes about the Silicon Valley stars and the entrepreneurial world. The week after that, I will be too busy with work and so on. I don't want Grandma lecturing me about my friends.

Chapter 19

I've been on several dates with Lora, and tonight we are hanging out at my place for the first time. She looks with curiosity at the books about Computer Science on my shelves. She suggests we watch one of her favorite inspirational films called *Magic Everywhere*. I agree because I want to be with her and be immersed in her world that feels so... magical. It's a little unusual—the film talks about how our thoughts impact the energy fields around us—but I'm enjoying the wine and the anticipation of what might happen.

A guy interviewed in the film talks about what to do to make dreams come true. "Imagine your dream as if it were already a reality. Imagine it in as much detail as possible." I try it out with my startup. I'm holding the Startup Incubator award—which in my fantasy, looks like an Oscar—feeling the weight and coolness of the metal in my hands. And now I am in my beautiful, sunlit rented office space, where I am running a business meeting with confidence and charisma. I'm looking at the members of my small but talented team sitting around the table, and when I turn my head to the right, Jack pops up next to me. What on earth is he doing there? I don't like that he automatically shows up in my startup dream. I am past that, and I can do it by myself. Okay, we did have a lot of fun, and it was super exciting to work with him on things, but that's enough. I erase him and try again, but no pleasant visualizations come to my mind anymore. I stop the exercise and try to follow the film again.

"Do you mind if I stay over tonight?" Lora asks unexpectedly.

Chapter 20

It's been a couple of weeks since I first slept with Lora, and she's been staying at my place about every other day. She is so feminine, so caring. I love listening to her and getting immersed in her world. I don't talk much when I'm with her, although she shows genuine interest in everything I have to say. We talked about my family and upbringing, but I haven't told her anything about my former friends, Jack, *Just City*, or the startup. Basically, she doesn't know about all the things that have been preoccupying me for so long.

The other day I was at Lora's when, after the long break, Adam texted me about a party he was planning and we exchanged a few updates about our internships. I didn't feel like telling Lora about the party—or going there myself, for that matter. Strangely, I don't want her to become part of my world—instead, I want to become part of hers. I also feel she might be disappointed if she learns more about me. I think she believes I'm much kinder than I actually am.

Lora is full of kindness for everything—animals, people, the "living Earth," as she calls it—and optimism. I almost feel envious when she talks about how the universe conspires to help her. Can it be true for me too? For a few days, I have been trying to see things a little bit like Lora does. In the morning, I would tell myself that it's going to be the best day of my life and that things would align in amazing ways, and man, the days have been really awesome. Alex praises me like hell at work, people are just super friendly everywhere, even in the streets, and at night, I land in the arms of this beautiful woman. I feel so happy...

Today is Saturday, and we don't have to get up early. Lora is lying next to me, her head on my shoulder, her beautiful red hair spread over my chest.

"You know I saw a ghost when I was a child."

I'm unsure if she is serious, so just in case, I ask without smiling, "What was it like?"

Lora describes this event in detail at the old house where her family used to live. I listen to her attentively, but I feel a slight unease. For a moment, I imagine sharing this with Grandma and her reaction, which probably would be full of scientific explanations. Frankly, I wouldn't argue because I never believed in ghosts. I don't know how to react or what to say. Luckily, I don't have to sit with these thoughts for too long. Lora mentions breakfast, and I change gears.

We spend the day together, but it feels a little bitter-sweet. I'm still imagining Grandma's reaction to the ghost story. I love Lora and her magical world but could I *live* in her world, so to speak? How much would be too much for me?

Chapter 21

O nly two weeks left of my summer internship, and all four of us—Lora, Maria, Alex, and I—are going to the meditation center today after Alex and I finish work. Two weeks of internship left also means two weeks before the deadline to apply to the New Entrepreneur Incubator. I can't believe it's so close! The money part is looking good. I can't imagine Alex not recommending me. My project has been great, and he has already praised me several times in front of the team. Our relationship outside work has only strengthened, and I consider him my friend. But the startup idea... man. Is it even realistic to come up with the idea and develop it enough for a convincing description in the application in just two weeks? I start feeling nervous.

Before the meditation session, I quickly look at the "How to Come Up with a Startup Idea" notes on my phone again: Identify Pain Points / Solve a Problem; Copy What Works; Use Your Skill Set; Get a Change of Scenery; Meditate.

Nothing has been working. Although meditation has been quite enlightening for how I see myself and others, even it hasn't been doing much to help with startup ideas. During the session today, I'm almost trying to force it: ideas, ideas, ideas... But it only causes frustration.

After the session, Maria asks me if I could meet with this spiritual healer woman. She says that as Lucy's god-father, there is a connection between the family and me, and she would greatly appreciate it if I chatted with the woman. A spiritual healer woman? I wonder what exactly I will be doing there... It does feel a little outside of my comfort zone... So—yes—as I immediately think about that list of ways to come up with a startup idea. That would be a definite change of scenery. I need to try something. Anything. I agree.

On the agreed-upon day, I go to see the healer woman. An average-sized woman in her fifties opens the door and invites me to come in. The apartment looks pretty nor-mal. I wasn't sure if I should expect a colorful cloth-cov-ered, incense-filled house, kind of what they show for psychics in movies, but the apartment appears to be quite modern, resembling Maria's apartment. In a strong Eastern European accent, she invites me to have some tea in the living room. As I scan the space and situation for potential startup ideas, the healer brings tea, asks me about my college studies and seems interested in what I say. She then asks me to sit on a chair in the middle of the room as she gets a small metallic frame with a handle with another smaller rotating frame inside the main structure. She holds this "antenna" next to me while continuing to chat about me and my family. I tell her that my parents don't live in the city, and my family here is basically my grandma, a neuroscience professor. I also tell her that I like participating in Grandma's scientific studies. I stop talking for a few minutes, but in my thoughts, I go back to the *Just City* game and the difficult experiences I had, feeling a bit sorry for myself.

The healer's cat walks into the room and jumps onto the chair where the woman sat while we had tea. She tells me stories about her cat and wraps up our session, thanking me for coming and asking if I'll see Maria the following day. She asks me to give Maria and Alex a home-baked cherry slab pie, which I agree to take.

It was obviously a strange experience. I'm not even sure what I "did" at this meeting. But I feel like I fulfilled my duty as a responsible godfather. No sign of great startup ideas, though. Nothing.

I take a route home that will take me past where the old homeless man hit me with the pipe. I feel the memories of the shock in my body... As I approach the place, I see the same guy, almost in the same spot, just sitting there and mumbling and laughing to himself. I walk past him and, not too far from him, see a younger man sitting on the pavement. His look is so thoughtful and sad, and lonely...? I slow down and, for a bit, watch how, on the opposite side of the sidewalk, a bunch of young street preachers announce on a portable loudspeaker that we're all going to hell without Jesus. The lead speaker urges the passersby to think about the salvation of the soul and maybe coincidentally points in the direction of the two homeless men every time he says the word "sinners." I look at the cherry pie in my hands, a pile of rectangular pieces on a tray covered with plastic wrap. I decide to ask the younger homeless man if he'd like a slice of a cherry pie. He says, "Sure, thank you, sir." I give him a piece. I then return to the old guy, cautiously approach him, and put a piece on the newspaper in front of him.

There must be resources that exist for them... Like a hotline or something... Hotline, right, and how will they find out about it and call it?

I look at the pie in my hand and go home, where I eat a nice meal, take a hot shower, and go to bed early.

Chapter 22

The next morning, I wake up with the idea of solar-powered tablets that can be given to homeless people to help them connect to the Internet and with quick links to resources. A video chat with a counselor who could talk to them, local medical assistance, and direct links to soup kitchens and shelters. What else?

I do some research and find the National Alliance to End Homelessness website, where I read "The solution to homelessness is simple—housing." Kind of obvious, but at the same time, it was embarrassingly non-obvious to me. The tablets will help people enter housing programs and when waiting is inevitable (and probably very, very long), all those immediate services can be accessed.

I feel so excited. Over the past weeks, the idea of participating in the startup competition was fading away—such different things were happening in my life, but this felt like a magical revelation. This is exactly what I want to pursue. And I can actually make a change in somebody's life.

Before going to my internship, I sketch the tablet's interface on an envelope lying on my kitchen counter. As I list the quick links, I can't help listing as the first one a link to a video chat with a live person (counselor, coordinator, volunteer—I don't know).

Nobody should be lonely. That's my wish for every person in the world. Since Mom read me the Corduroy book when I was a child, I had this wish.

I start to feel a bit of Lora's magic, which gives me the feeling that everything will fall into place.

As I keep sketching the ideas, I think about one of my *Just City* lives as a homeless person and its tragic ending. A separate quick link to a Suicide Prevention Hotline. Definitely. I think one can dial *9-8-8*. I must find out. I would also need to find some kind of a local clinic for medical care in general. Where can they go if they are sick? And, of course, a food bank! The clinic and food bank must be local, and I will need to find collaborators and get letters of support. I know we have a food bank in the city, so I search for it and discover that they have ongoing opportunities for volunteering—sorting food and stuff like that—in the evenings and on weekends. I sign up for a few hours of volunteering for the following evening. This way, I can better understand how it can be linked to the... "Street Angel." This will be the name of the tablets for the homeless.

I know if I don't pull myself away now, I will never make it to work on time.

Chapter 23

Volunteering at the Food Bank feels terrific. Doing simple physical work, such as sorting plums, is pleasantly different from my usual office work, sitting at a desk and staring at a computer for hours. I didn't know I could use a break for my brain. My supervisor is very friendly and during breaks is always happy to answer my questions about the process of distributing food to people in need. He introduces me to the director, Ben. Ben is obviously a visual information processing type. We have a conversation in his tiny office plastered with all kinds of flyers and printouts of articles. I describe my idea and show him the envelope with the sketched interface. He seems to like my Street Angel and the envelope sketch. Hearing from someone who doesn't even know me that my idea could be extremely helpful feels good. We discuss how we could work together and if Ben could write a letter of support for my startup competition. As I'm about to head out of the smallest office I've been to, I glance at the papers covering the door. Next to an info sheet about what food expiration dates actually mean, an article's title reads, "Being Homeless Should Not Be a Crime." Oh my goodness, it is?!

I quickly turn around, borrow Ben's pen, and add an icon for a pro bono legal assistance quick link to my sketch on the envelope.

When I'm at Lora's the following evening, I decide to share the whole startup story with her. Well, not the whole story. I'm not going to tell her about Jack, our original startup idea to stop the homeless from stealing shopping carts—which Lora would probably find brutal—and my fight with Jack. Just the good part that starts now. This way, I can share a little more about myself and not disappoint her at the same time.

"Remember that tarot card reading you did for me?" I ask her as she is making a   vegetarian dinner for us.

"Of course."

"You never asked what I had in mind."

"Well, actually, you are not supposed to tell me."

"Can I tell you that yesterday I met with the director of the Food Bank, and I'm thinking about working with them on a project to help facilitate services for homeless people? I want to found a startup that would make solar-powered tablets that can be given to homeless people to help them connect with assistance hotlines, local medical and food services, and housing programs." Lora is listening attentively, her eyes widened. I hope it's a sign of excitement, not disapproval. I continue, "It will be called

'Street Angel.' I mean, I'm not sure if it will work out, and I have many open questions..."

"Oh my God, Nathan! This is fascinating!"

Lora hugs me, and I feel the warmth of her support.

"This is so exciting! So, so, so, wonderful." Lora pauses and smiles. "You said you would connect them to medical services. I happen to know some people who run a wonderful alternative medicine center; they are real healers! You should talk to them. I'll be happy to connect you!"

I feel a little unprepared, as I thought about talking to my grandma because she knows people at Magnus University Clinic. "That's so nice of you to offer," I say and pause, trying to quickly assess if that would be the right way to go.

Lora continues, probably thinking my response was a yes, "Oh, you know what else you could do? Offer homeless people some classes, some program to teach them how to manifest what they desire in their lives."

Lora sounds so enthusiastic. It makes me think about my own experimentation with changing my thinking and how things really seemed to improve. But I feel uneasy. Maybe it makes sense for Lora and me to try to "think things into reality," but I think about the homeless people I saw, and I feel this mismatch... There should be real policies and programs to help the homeless, not a talk on how to *manifest* their desires.

Lora is looking at me inquisitively. She is so supportive, I don't want to be a jerk and make her feel bad. I decide to go with her first suggestion, which sounds less out there... "So, a medical center? You can really put me in touch with them?"

"Of course! Dr. Lena is an amazing homeopath, and their medical center is such an energetically beautiful place! I'll ask her if maybe we can come by tomorrow evening."

"Wonderful!" I reply, trying to smile and hoping she forgot her other idea. A memory of Grandma's lecture on homeopathy is trying to surface in my head, but I decide not to go there.

The alternative medicine center reminds me of the meditation center, except that there is a wall of jars with herbs behind the receptionist.

I look at the receptionist and immediately recognize Tim, with whom I went to high school for a year. I think I was fourteen. He had to repeat that year more than once, and I've heard he never finished high school—he aged out and couldn't graduate.

"Tim!" I exclaim.

"Nathan!" His calm facial expression becomes lively.

"Dr. Lena is ready to see you," Tim greets Lora and points down the hallway. "The first door to the right."

"Catch up with you in a bit!" I say to Tim and follow Lora to see Dr. Lena.

Tim and I weren't big friends at school, and I mostly remember him due to an episode that left a bad feeling in me. One morning I was rushing to school, excited to present my answers to twenty riddles we were given a few days earlier by our math teacher for extra credit. We were allowed to discuss them with other students or work in teams, but I immediately knew the answers to most of them, and the remaining few I cracked by myself using my special doodling techniques. Seriously. The last one went something like, "A taxi driver is going the opposite way down a one-way street. He passes five policemen along the way, none of whom stops him. Why not?" I remember struggling with that one, but after sketching it, I realized that the riddle tricked me by focusing on the person's occupation—but it never said the person was engaged in that occupation at the time. The answer was simple: Because the taxi driver was walking!

Anyway, on the way to school, I noticed Tim walking slowly. As I approached him, I asked, "What's up?" It turned out that his father got very sick two days earlier, and they had to go to the hospital. Naturally, Tim didn't do anything for school.

"Did you do the riddles?" Tim asked me. If I said yes, I knew he would ask me to tell him the answers. So I mumbled, "No." I didn't feel like sharing my answers, so I lied. I know he failed the class, and rumor had it that that failed class became the last straw making him repeat the year. To avoid feeling bad about myself, I kept telling myself that it would not be fair to share the answers with him. Tim was not a good student. Even if he hadn't spent the last two days with his sick father, he wouldn't have gotten the answers himself. *I did the right thing*. I kept telling myself. *It's only fair. I deserved that extra credit, he didn't.* Even worse, I'm now reluctantly starting to remember that on a few occasions, when the situation presented itself, I told other students that Tim didn't know even the simplest things and didn't deserve to move to the next grade. This probably worsened Tim's already poor reputation and made me feel more right. I managed to convince myself and it worked for a long time, but now, all I feel is guilt.

Dr. Lena listens to me tell her about my Street Angel idea and says their center would be happy to collaborate. She says she would ask Tim to help with the project: prepare the letter of support for my startup competition application and other things I may need.

Lora and I return to the reception and chat with Tim. I describe what the letters of support are expected to contain. I look at the jars with herbs and wonder if that's what the homeless people would need. And how about insurance? Does Medicaid even cover all this? Man... I feel uncomfortable asking Tim more questions. I have that riddle story in my head... I wonder if he remembers. He probably found out that I got the extra credit...I'm not sure. Maybe it wasn't that bad anyway, him not finishing high school. Look, after all, he has a job and looks pretty content. But I would hate to mislead him again and back out of this collaboration.

Lora looks so happy and upbeat, and I don't dare to share my doubts about the center, let alone the riddle story. Well, at least I'll have a letter of support for my application on such short notice. Time is running out.

Chapter 24

On Friday, I give the final presentation at work. I still have one week of the internship left, and hopefully, I'll keep working after that. The presentation goes really well, and after work, we have a little celebration with Alex and some other colleagues. We hang out at the café. Maria and little Lucy join, as well as Lora. Everyone is hugging, even my colleagues and the girls who hadn't met each other before; everyone is so warm and nice. I haven't seen little Lucy in a while because she's been sick. She cries more than usual, and I tell Maria I'm happy to hold Lucy if she likes.

As I hold Lucy, she seems to have a fever and a strange cough. "Have you been to the doctor?" I ask. Maria says that they have but doesn't say much more. For a second, I wonder if maybe Lucy got one of those childhood diseases because of not being vaccinated, but I decide to keep it to myself in order not to upset Maria.

I later give a little speech, saying how this experience with the summer internship was really great and how awesome it was to meet all of them. I have a strong feeling Alex will tell me that I get the contract to continue working with them. He seems pleased with my work, and our relationship is so good. It's kind of crazy, but just in a short time, I became his niece's godfather and his friend's boyfriend. Alex raises his beer and says, "Nathan, to you! It's been great working with you, and I hope we'll see each other again. Cheers!" Hmm... Does that mean he'll recommend me or not? I feel a little disappointed. I know the decision is not due until next week, but I thought it was a perfect moment to mention that he is 100% recommending me, and I would then get paid the advance on September 1. I get another beer and try not to think about it.

We talk about meditation retreats. The other colleagues leave after about an hour. Maria starts talking about abundance in one's life and how one should balance energies to achieve it. I think about the homeless people I met and struggle to apply what Maria says to them. Would the balance of spiritual energies keep them from freezing or starving? Maria continues talking about the teachings of one guru she has met: "So there are 121 chakras. Two of them are just outside the body..."

I remember Grandma holding the brain model, explaining how damage to the tissue changes who we are. In my imagination, I try to attach two chakras on top of the brain and can't help but slightly shake my head, finding little sense in this. Maybe the disappointment with Alex's silence or the beer makes me jump into the conversation. "How does he know there are exactly that many?" I try to say it jokingly.

Maria pauses. For a moment, it appears like she is trying to come up with an answer but can't. Finally, she must have found the right answer and says confidently but calmly, "Look, the need of your mind to question everything is what stands between you and peace."

I remember our meditation teacher saying something similar once, and back then, I kind of dug it. Not right now, though. Isn't this reply just avoiding my legitimate question? I remember Alex talking the other day about dogma and how he is against it. I kept thinking about this word, "dogma," over the past weeks, and now I feel like there is this contradiction... They keep saying it's so important to be open-minded, and I have been. So why am I not allowed to ask this question?

"But isn't that dogmatic? I mean that I can't even question this guru's statement about chakras?" I try to sound calm but serious. After half a minute of silence, it starts feeling awkward. No one thinks my question is addressed to them, including Maria. I realize I don't want to turn this celebration into a serious debate and decide not to push further. Thankfully, Lora announces she wants to order a pie, and we talk about the delicious cherry pie the healer woman gave to Maria and Alex.

"By the way, what was the result of her readings?" I ask, remembering the whole unusual experience of going to see her.

"She did link Lucy's current health problems to you," Maria says calmly.

"What?! Lucy's health problems are because of me?" Is she saying it just because she is mad at my chakra question? She does seem to mean it; she looks calm and matter-of-fact.

"Yeah, but don't worry about it," Maria replies.

"Don't worry about it? What do you mean? What... what else did she say? What should I be doing?"

"Well," she says. "One should live cleanly."

"What does that mean?!" I'm shocked. I don't understand what it is about. How could I have possibly made Lucy sick? It seems to be some kind of whooping cough or something.

"That's all she said. She did some rituals. Don't worry too much about it. I'm sure Lucy will get well soon."

I don't find any words to say and just try to normalize my breathing as Maria changes the topic, as if nothing happened. I feel confused and even angry. I look at Alex, and he just calmly stares at me. Does he agree with it? Does he take it seriously? What does it even mean? How can I be responsible for Lucy's health problems? And what does it mean to "live cleanly?" What am I supposed to change? Am I not loving enough? I'm definitely much more loving than I used to be! Is it because of my past? Or is it because I don't necessarily share all of their beliefs?

After we leave the café, I walk Lora home, and before saying goodbye, I ask her if she believes in what the healer woman said.

"Oh Nathan, don't take it so personally."

"How can I not take it personally? Why would she say it? If Maria didn't believe it, why would she say it to me?"

Lora tries to kiss me, but I'm completely preoccupied with what happened.

"Wouldn't it bother you if you heard something like that about you? What would you do?" I ask Lora.

"You could try to take her advice."

"What advice? To live 'cleanly?' What does it even mean? And how can it be that something I do affects the health of a child I'm not even related to?" I can't keep my voice level.

"She is our goddaughter, and we are connected on a spiritual level."

"What level is it?"

Lora looks at me, then to the side, and doesn't give me an answer.

Frustrated, I decide to call it an evening. I briefly kiss Lora good night and head home.

I feel broken. Again. My loving and caring friends are now accusing me of being a bad spiritual influence on this little child... Are they accusing me of being a bad person? How do they even decide that? Okay, the healer *read* it, but they believe it! Is it because I said something critical of their spiritual stuff? Maybe I never really bought into their "supernatural beliefs," as Grandma would probably call it... Or did I ever say anything to them about vaccination after my conversation with Grandma? No, I didn't. Although now I think that maybe Lucy is sick because of not getting vaccinated—who knows? Perhaps I just didn't do enough for Lucy as her godfather? I don't know... It's all too crazy!

And what if Alex doesn't recommend me for the job now?

Chapter 25

On Saturday morning, I call Grandma and ask if I can come over for tea. I've been avoiding meeting with her for a while, but now I need to come clean and tell her about my disappointing experience with my new friends. As soon as I get inside, she asks me how I am and whether I'm okay.

"Not so great, Grandma..." I sit down and lay my arms on the dining table.

I tell her the whole story in a cumbersome way as we wait for the kettle to boil for tea. I jump back and forth, telling her about Maria, Lucy, Alex, and Lora. I'm still feeling distraught.

"Let me see if I understand it correctly, Nathan," Grandma says after quietly listening to me. "It looks like Maria is falsely accusing you of negatively affecting the health of your goddaughter based purely on supernatural beliefs."

"That sums it up pretty well." I sigh, feeling a little relieved that she knows what happened, even though all this shows she was right all along, being suspicious about my new friends. I like that she uses the word "falsely."

"I'm so sorry, my dear! It's so unfair. It's pure nonsense." She looks at me sympathetically.

"I guess you can say *I told you so.*" I'm replaying in my head the first unpleasant conversation with Grandma when I had just met Alex and Maria and went to the meditation center, and then her lecture about "supernatural beliefs."

"Oh no, Nathan. That was so wrong of me. I felt terrible after our last conversation. I want to apologize."

"You had reasons to say those things. I guess I should have listened better."

"I promised myself not to impose my views on anyone, but on that day, I broke my own promise... I had no right to say those things about your friends... and at that point, they hadn't done anything to hurt you."

"Well, now they have... You know, when I started hanging out with them, I felt like I belonged. They are so kind and caring. I felt so lucky to have such loving people for my friends and my girlfriend," I say to Grandma. "It's like people are either jerks or crazy."

"One can be kind without believing in bizarre things." Grandma starts preparing tea.

"I don't know; it doesn't seem to be the case. I tried Dad's approach, being rational. That didn't go well. I tried a more loving way, which led me to... ghosts and stuff."

I shake my head, take a few hazelnuts from a bowl, and start lining them up on the table.

"Well, I think your dad confuses rationality with self-ishness. The latter is a value one can choose or not choose for oneself. Rationality, reason, is something entirely different: Like science, it's simply an error-reduction method that helps us find the best approximation to the truth." Grandma puts two cups of tea on the table, sits down, and looks at my line of hazelnuts with a slight smile. "You know, the truth doesn't care whether you believe in it or not. In our shared reality, there should always be only one true answer if we are talking about facts. Very different from personal values! My values can be different from yours, whereas there is no 'my truth' or 'your truth.' It's so important not to confuse values with facts. But do you know what the best part is? You don't have to choose one or the other: being loving or being rational! Or, as Professor Sapolsky once said, 'You don't have to choose between being scientific and being compassionate.' I would even say, on the contrary, your ability to understand the world as close to what it is as possible, without the confirmation bias and preferences, gives you the ability to be truly compassionate and not self-centered."

I have this strong feeling that Grandma is right. At the same time, Grandma calls all those things my friends believe in "bizarre..." And, yes, some of them are too much for me, but many other things I discovered thanks to them have been amazing. I feel they got me out of that dark place after my fight with Jack.

"But all those things Maria, Alex, and Lora talk about seem to work: meditation, connecting to higher self... I felt it, Grandma!"

"They do work, but *for a different reason*. There is nothing supernatural about getting amazing clarity and feelings of calm, or even physically recovering from meditation or even from imagining chakras, angels, etc. Symbolic imagery, metaphors, and rituals are *very* powerful because we are evolutionarily very susceptible to them. Our minds tend to make predictions and then use our internal 'pharmacies' to make ourselves feel better or recover from illnesses to some degree—that's what we call the placebo effect."

"So, can I keep using those things for my well-being?"

"Of course. You can and should if it works for you!"

"But would it still work if I knew those are just metaphors? Not actual reality?"

"Yes, they could. There have been studies of open-label placebos that show how if you give a person a pill and say that it is a placebo, basically, an inert substance, and you even print PLACEBO on the label, it still works for many conditions. Especially if you give the person an explanation of how it works and why it may work for them. By 'works,' I, of course, always mean the average, statistically significant effect obtained in randomized-controlled trials. Confirmed by independent research groups. That's what 'evidence-based' means in medicine and many other sciences."

"Wow, that's crazy." Thinking about how all those "magical" things work precisely and only because they are believed in fascinates me. "So, Maria's, Lora's, and others' beliefs are real, in a way, as some kind of self-fulfilling prophecy?"

"Yes, but the bottom line is that *there is always an explanation*." Grandma sounds very convincing.

It makes so much sense... I did have doubts about my friends' views of things and how things work. Lora's ghosts... Maria's energies... But what am I supposed to do now? With them and with the alternative medicine center? I'll need to deal with that one very quickly. It feels clear to me now: I don't want to have non-scientific partners for my startup. Placebo sounds nice, but I can't rely on it to help the homeless. You can't placebo away hunger, homelessness, or epidemics...

"If I needed a provider of evidence-based medicine for my project, who would it be?" I ask Grandma, understanding that I need to change my plans.

"The University Clinic."

"Do you know anyone there I could talk to about collaboration?"

"Of course!"

I decide to finally tell Grandma about my startup idea. She listens carefully without commenting much on it. As soon as I'm done, she eagerly sends a couple of emails to her contact people at Magnus University Clinic. I feel so safe and supported—Grandma having my back like that despite everything. I know, of course, that would mean turning away the alternative center and talking to Tim... I already feel so guilty. What if I just get the support letter from the University Clinic and let it fade away with Tim? I know that won't feel right. I probably will let him know somehow...

Lora texts me and asks if we can meet. I text back that I'm at Grandma's.

"Grandma, do you need help with anything today?" I ask, hoping it will delay going home and having to answer Lora and meeting with her. I'm not ready to talk to her now. I need to think about what to do after what happened.

"Yes! Actually, I'm going to the University now to set up and test all the equipment for my *Just City* lecture on Thursday. I'm meeting with a technical assistant at 11 a.m., but your help would be even better. We will have three stations for a live game demo before and after the lecture, so we want to test everything today. I know you are good with all this VR equipment."

"Yes!" I'm surprised Grandma has a concrete need for my help. I asked her for my own—let's be honest—selfish reason. Would she have asked me otherwise? Maybe I should try offering to help a little more often.

When we arrive at the central campus of Magnus University, James Building, Grandma unlocks a huge amphitheater-shaped lecture hall and turns on the lights. The tech arrives a few minutes later and brings three computers. I help him set up the VR units while Grandma tests the microphone and her slides on the huge screen. She walks to different spots in the lecture hall, testing how things look on the screen. At some point, she sits in the center of the middle section of the descending rows of chairs and stays there for a while, looking at one of her slides on the screen.

My earlier realization about how self-focused I am comes to mind. In all my conversations with Grandma, it's always been about me. I feel a little guilty about that. What is she thinking and feeling, sitting there by herself? I imagine for a moment as if I were her, looking at the screen showing the results of her work. That must be a big moment for her.

The tech leaves to get different connectors, and I go down the stairs and sit next to Grandma.

"You are preparing really well for your lectures."

"I don't always do as much, but this project is very important to me."

"Can I ask you something?"

"Sure."

"Why did it bother you so much from the beginning when I started hanging out with my new friends and going to the meditation center? You said something about it reminding you of something or someone else. What was it?"

Grandma tells me about her authoritarian upbringing. Her father was very dogmatic. He once had 'a divine revelation' and therefore was convinced that he was always right and that everyone must obey. Her freedom of thought was suppressed by him when she was growing up. Out of rebellion, she became a scientist.

"Only later I realized the extent of his horrible actions…" Grandma presses her lips together and looks up. Is she crying? "Things he did to suppress objections by anyone, including his children, to his 'divine truth' were horrendous."

I can't help my curiosity. "Things like…?"

"Like washing my sister's mouth with bleach for disagreeing." Grandma's eyes widen, and she stares straight in front of her. I feel a shiver running down my spine. Her older sister is my real grandma, whom I never met because she died shortly after giving birth to my mom.

Grandma finally blinks and lowers her head. "Voltaire once said, 'Those who can make you believe absurdities can make you commit atrocities.'" She pauses, and I notice that she makes fists with her hands. "That's when I promised to do everything I could to promote critical, objective thinking in people. I also promised myself never to impose my views on others. Giving others the freedom to think and decide for themselves is extremely important. That's why I can't apologize enough for how I reacted to your friends."

"Oh no, Grandma," I immediately say, deeply impacted by her story. It takes me a few seconds to remember her first reaction to my sharing about my friends. "Well, it wasn't really as much about my friends. It's more that it made me feel like you don't see me as mature, as a grownup."

"Oh, I am so sorry I made you feel that way, Nathan. Nothing can be further from the truth!"

I realize we switched the topic to me again, so I ask her, "Did you... did you forgive your father?"

Grandma looks down. "It still hurts... I wish I had done something to protect my sister. The atrocities committed by my father and those being committed all over the world by so many people... It's so hard to accept it. But a scientific view of things can also help see the impersonal nature of what is being done. The more fully one understands the objective reality of the human mind and behavior, the easier it is to see the true meaning of forgiveness: There is nothing to forgive, for those 'connectomes' don't understand what they are doing."

I look at her, amazed at how much she cares. I had no idea. I notice tears on her cheeks.

I think about Grandma's life experience and how passionate she is about what she has learned and her work.

"So, is *Just City* an expression of the life view you told me about?"

"Definitely! One of my two 'big projects.' The other is a highly unpopular course on Critical Thinking for youth that I piloted, but nobody wants to implement." She looks at me and smiles.

"Really?" I smile back.

"But I'll keep trying!"

The tech comes back, and we finish the setup.

Later, on my way home, I think about how Grandma's life motto drives her work and about what happened to my old life motto... So many things have happened, and I think I've gained so many insights, but I still don't see it. I don't know how to put my new understanding of things into words, into guidelines for myself.

Chapter 26

At home, I eat lunch, still thinking about the life mottos of people I know and my own. I find Grandma's website and look to see if I can find her Critical Thinking course. Maybe it can help me understand how people determine and live by certain principles. Here it is. It says it's a pilot, and now it's mostly a collection of links to different content, some of it even behind paywalls. The intro to the course is a four-minute video I decide to watch right away.

The video starts with a depiction of the Earth, accompanied by mesmerizing music and a deep narrator's voice, slowly but passionately talking to me.

"Consider again that pale blue dot we've been talking about..." The sound is deep in my headset. *"Imagine you are staring at the dot for any length of time and then try to convince yourself that God created the whole universe for only one of the 10 million or so species of life that inhabit that speck of dust. Now take it a step further. Imagine that everything was made just for a single shade of that species,*

or gender, or ethnic or religious subdivision." The narrator goes on to say how we humans tend to *project our own nature onto nature* and how limited our ability to understand the world is. He then quotes Darwin, who wrote, *"Man in his arrogance thinks himself a great work worthy of the interposition of a deity… More humble, and I think truer to consider him created from animals."*

The narrator continues to say how we humans, who emerged from microbes, don't have control of our thoughts and feelings, and, *"On top of all this, we're making a mess of our planet and becoming a danger to ourselves. The trapdoor beneath our feet swings open. We find ourselves in bottomless free fall. If it takes a little myth and ritual to get us through a night that seems endless, who among us cannot sympathize and understand? We long to be here for a purpose, even though, despite much self-deception, none is evident."*

I immediately think of the "myths and rituals" and the whole supernatural worldview of my friends… And about the fact that there is no evidence for any events that don't obey physical laws or for any "bigger" purpose, or that the universe "conspires to help us," as Lora says.

"The significance of our lives and our fragile planet is then determined only by our own wisdom and courage. We are the custodians of life's meaning. We long for a Parent to care for us, to forgive us our errors, to save us from our childish mistakes. But knowledge is preferable to ignorance. Better by far to embrace the hard truth than a reassuring fable.

Modern science has been a voyage into the unknown, with a lesson in humility waiting at every stop. Our commonsense intuitions can be mistaken. Our preferences don't count. We do not live in a privileged reference frame. If we crave some cosmic purpose, then let us find ourselves a worthy goal."

I feel chills and read the comment to the video: "A Reassuring Fable" from *Pale Blue Dot: A Vision of the Human Future in Space* by Carl Sagan.

I rewatch the video a few times, addicted to the music and the depth of the message.

It sounds like it is completely up to me, up to everyone, to "find ourselves a worthy goal..." It sounds like so much freedom but also so much responsibility.

The rest of the Critical Thinking course links to various lectures on biology, neuroscience, psychology, philosophy, philosophy of science, etc. I start watching them and feel amazed at how different they are from my regular university lectures. They force you to think. They bring *aha* moments and sometimes a kind of shock. In one of them, the professor sits cross-legged on a desk, telling the students about death. He elaborately and convincingly demonstrates how there is no good reason to posit the existence of an immaterial soul and, therefore, to expect an afterlife. Given this, he discusses whether suicide can ever be rational. Other lectures talk about evolution and biology, and how organisms evolved in a way that increases the probability of their survival and propagation but how there is never a "purpose" in evolution, and how wrong it is to say ,"They evolved so that they..." There is no "so that;" there is only "because." A specific feature, like a long neck, was beneficial for survival; that is why animals with such a feature due to random genetic mutations were more likely to survive and have offspring. Everything we see is the result of this mechanism and not of some divine intention. This, of course, includes humans, which makes us very non-special.

Moreover, although we clearly shouldn't search for sentience (the ability to have feelings such as pain, pleasure, and suffering) in crystals that don't even have a nervous system, we shouldn't think that humans are the only sentient animals. Other lectures remind me more of my grandma's speeches about cognitive biases and how we err... They teach how to recognize the tricks our minds play on us and teach things like "the Fine Art of Baloney Detection." Man, I easily remember so many things my friends, parents, teachers, news anchors, politicians—almost anyone around me—have said.

I'm especially fascinated by Occam's Razor principle, saying that when faced with two hypotheses that explain the data equally well, one should choose the simpler one that makes the fewest assumptions. There can be a fallen tree that doesn't look ill. So, one explanation is that the wind was really strong last night, and another is that a mystical creature came and pushed it... Another example: A person seems to make others feel bad next to them even if that person doesn't say anything. Why?

Micro expressions, gestures, and posture that convey that person's psychological state to others, or the "aura" and "energies" that are being "sensed" by others?

Similarly, the "burden of proof" concept says that the person making a claim (such as a claim about auras and energies) must provide sufficient supporting evidence for that claim. It's not your obligation to prove that there are no auras or energies. Or, in the words of Carl Sagan, "Extraordinary claims require extraordinary evidence."

Man, I wish I had such a clear and, well, let's call it rational (in the correct meaning of the word) approach earlier. I would have maybe discussed it with Lora when she told me about ghosts. Would she be open to discussing what else could have explained what she saw?

Another whole lecture on conspiracy theories, debunking some common ones and explaining what drives our belief in them, but acknowledging some real conspiracies that happened in history.

And at some point, I realize that it's midnight, and I've been snacking on pita chips, probably only thanks to them going on for so long without dinner.

Before going to bed, I decide to share the links to the lectures on Reddit, where I'm rarely active. I secretly hope Lora will watch them and understand how and why our minds tend to fall into the supernatural trap.

As I'm falling asleep, the ideas from the lectures merge into this exciting feeling of realizing something important, something very valuable about how the world works.

In the morning, I get a text from Lora asking if I would come to her place today. I go on Reddit to check if she watched any of the lectures, but she didn't. Instead, to my surprise, I notice that in addition to some of my other friends who liked and commented on a lecture here and there, ALL of the lectures I shared were liked by Jack.

I'm feeling perplexed and, I guess, pleasantly surprised. Did he really watch all of them? Did he stay up to watch them? Why? We haven't talked since the fight or, more precisely, since he told me he was applying for the start-up competition without me.

I know that Jack always dug the reason part of critical thinking. It's the kindness and compassion part that's a little problem here. Why do my friends seem to be either from one camp or the other? Grandma says you don't need to choose between the two, but why do all my friends choose one and stick to it?

I get back to Lora's text. I still feel uncertain about what to do about our relationship, but I can't just be ghosting her. No pun intended. I reply that I'll come over in the evening.

I look at Lora's breathtaking profile photo on Reddit and see that she was active, sharing and commenting last night and this morning, but not on my lectures. I briefly look over the shared lectures and think about how much sense they make and how exciting it is to feel like

I understand the world better. At the same time, I feel this almost painful disappointment that I won't be able to share the excitement with Lora because it's not the type of thing she cares for, at least now.

I remember her reaction to Maria's accusations and saying I should live "cleanly." On Friday, it made me angry. Now, it makes me sad. What makes people just believe things? It makes me think of witch burnings in old times. Okay, maybe my case is not as bad, but it is as unfair and unfounded. Grandma's confession and that phrase about people who believe absurdities and how such people can commit atrocities... I don't think Lora, Maria, or Alex would ever commit atrocities. Probably, at most, they'd not vaccinate a child and blame a friend for the child's sickness. I'm obviously still trying to figure out things myself. This summer has been a rollercoaster in terms of my worldview. But it feels like there is a canyon between us. Our worldviews are just too different...

It becomes clear to me that I have just decided to break up with Lora.

———◦———

When I see Lora in the evening, I remember how attracted to her I am. I miss her smell, her smile, and her uplifting presence. She is so beautiful... Does it matter that we have different worldviews?

Before we start making dinner together, I tell her about my decision.

She reacts in a surprisingly easy way. She takes my hands, looks into my eyes, and says, "If you think we shouldn't see each other anymore, then probably it's for the best." She seems to be satisfied with the reason about the different worldviews. I told her the truth.

It feels a little suspicious how easy it is for her. Maybe she wanted to break up with me herself? I ask her if she is okay (because she does look okay), and she explains that she believes in destiny, and if we break up, it means we were supposed to.

As we make our last dinner together, Lora looks calm and focused. I cut vegetables for a salad as she cooks mushroom ravioli. She must have expected the end of our relationship or planned it herself. Obviously. When setting up the table, Lora tries to squeeze in the salad bowl between the plates, and one of them falls on the floor and breaks. Lora, the embodiment of optimism and positive outlook, starts crying as she picks up the broken pieces. I help her in silence and decide that maybe I shouldn't jump to conclusions about what she does or doesn't feel. What do I know, after all?

We still decide to spend the night together. I embrace Lora and hide my face in her hair, which is falling down her shoulders. I breathe in deeply, smelling her hair. Why can't I just stay with her? Who cares about supernatural beliefs? I ask myself rhetorically. I don't need an answer. I know that I care.

Chapter 27

The next morning, I go to work directly from Lora's place after giving her a warm embrace and saying goodbye. I feel light sadness, like when the warm season of the year ends. I know this wasn't the right relationship, but will I ever find the right one?

The startup competition deadline is on Friday, and Alex's memo says he's not even going to be in the office today. I'm finishing up my final report for the summer internship, not clear if there will be any continuation. My report is looking good, and man, I did such good work. Should I email him and ask? I feel nervous. I may have ruined everything at the celebration on Friday... I tried to get closer to Alex to get the job offer and the money, and instead, I got too close. I should have just kept my distance.

Should I call Alex and tell him that I take all my words about questioning chakras back? Tell him that Lucy's health problems are not my fault?

What am I supposed to do? With the funding, with Tim, with Alex? I need some principles to guide me through such decisions, like a formula. I'll go to Grandma's tonight and ask her about how she came up with hers.

———◦———

Grandma seems happy I came to have dinner with her on a Monday. I tell her that I watched her course on critical thinking and that it is outstanding. Her face shines. As I'm helping her set the table, I start a conversation about life principles, hoping she can give me a recipe on how to come up with a clear set of those.

"Grandma, you told me that you have a set of life principles..."

"And how I broke some of them with you? How I shouldn't have said what I did to you about your friends?"

"No, no. I want to ask you how I can come up with life principles to guide my actions."

"Oh, I'm not sure about the actual process. It's just that my early life events shaped the way I think, and the principles kind of emerged from it. I have never deviated from them since then. Well, with some exceptions..."

I sigh. "I see." This doesn't sound like step-by-step instructions. I'll have to figure it out myself.

I remember that I had a set of principles before. They came about in a similar way, so I understand. But something else bothers me about what Grandma said. I start feeling this discomfort because what I'm trying to do is to come up with a new life credo after abandoning the old one.

"Grandma, I used to have a set of principles but then… I changed my mind. Is it a sign of weakness?" I ask.

"Nathan, just as in science, changing your mind if your knowledge is updated is not a bad thing, but a very good, very important thing. This is what being grown up means to me." She says it with emphasis and looks at me. "I'm proud of you."

As we eat dinner, we chat about light stuff, but my thoughts keep going back to what she said about the meaning of being grown up, and I feel elated.

Before leaving her house, I walk into her study and sit on the couch, staring at the Free Will painting again. The beautiful, brown-eyed woman with a small marionette in her hand, a mini-version of her.

"Grandma, what is this painting really about?"

"About 10 years ago, Mark painted it after several long discussions I had with him about free will. What do you think it means?"

"Mark painted it? You never told me that." Mark, Grandma's friend, is an academic, so this is a surprise. "Well, she is choosing and directing her own behavior… Some kind of metacognition. She is really beautiful. The frame seems a little too small, though."

"You think it's a coincidence?"

"What do you mean?" I'm trying to imagine what Mark was thinking, squeezing the painting into the tight frame. The beautiful woman looks so calm, confident, and even powerful, manipulating her marionette's actions. Is it a deception?

"Well, she is constrained by the frame."

I suddenly see it. "Is the point to say that even though we choose our actions all the time, the 'chooser' hasn't chosen themselves? The stuff you keep talking about?"

"You got it."

"So basically, there is no free will on a deep level… Physics determines everything. But does it matter in everyday life that there is no free will in this deep sense? In our perception, we still have to decide what to do every day?" I ask, thinking about all the decisions I must make about my startup.

"Good question. It doesn't seem to matter for your everyday decisions and actions—and there still seems to be this almost overwhelming freedom of choices of what to do and how to be. It definitely feels like we have free will. There is, however, deep importance to remembering that it's not true so we don't sink into the delusion of 'I would have never done that' or 'I couldn't have fallen that low,' and so forth. Basically, remembering that part can allow people to have more compassion and not separate themselves as much from others, as if they had some kind of special little godly soul that descended into their body, and that's who they truly are. With all the excuses and understanding they have for their own little soul but a canyon of separation from others. We are all just our connectomes."

None of this would have made sense a few months ago, but now I understand.

I look at the painting for some time, thinking again about how beautiful the woman is. This brings me to the painting's creator.

"So, really, Mark painted it?"

"Yes, he is extremely talented."

"So, what's up with you two?"

"We are good friends."

"He means much more to you, doesn't he?"

Grandma is quiet, and I realize that I'm right.

"Have you told him that?"

"We agreed not to have any strings attached to our relationship, and I respect his freedom," Grandma says with a wistful smile.

"What do you mean? What does not telling him have to do with freedom?"

"He doesn't need my feelings being imposed on him. We have an agreement."

"But wasn't it like a decade ago? He would still be free to decide what to do with the information. Maybe he's changed his mind. People change. You don't know what's going on with him. What if he feels the same way you do but is afraid to tell you?"

She becomes even quieter, so I wrap up the conversation. What do I know, after all?

Before going out the door, I look at Grandma and say, "By the way, Grandma, I prefer you to tell me your opinions openly. Even if it looks like I don't."

She smiles.

"And I think you should talk to Mark."

"Go," she says and smiles again.

At home, not having received any specific advice from Grandma, I open a new document on my computer and write, "My Life Code." I sit for about five minutes staring at it. There is this emptiness, like when I tried to come up with the startup idea. Speaking of which, why don't I keep working on developing the design of the hardware and software for my solar-powered tablets? Although I don't have to have the prototype for my submission on Friday, I think the more details I have thought through, the better I can fine-tune my application.

I get so engrossed in my work that when I briefly look at emails and see one from Alex, I don't feel an urge to read it. I still do, and in it he asks me to come into the office around noon on Thursday to discuss my final report and finalize my internship's completion: close my accounts, etc. It slowly dawns on me that it is basically the final "No" from him regarding continuing my work at the company and getting the money. I feel that strange sense of relief when something you were afraid of happening finally does. I know it's an important development, but

I'm so excited about developing the specs and shaping up my tablet that I don't have time to mull it over. I stay up until 2 a.m. working.

Chapter 28

W hen I wake up in the morning, I feel excited about my progress on the tablet. I have specs for the compact solar power kit built into the tablet's cover, the operating system, and an Internet-for-everyone satellite connection. I decide to savor that, so I sit down and meditate.

My eyes are closed, but I sense the light from the rising sun on my eyelids. I think about the different types of meditation I learned at the meditation center, like focusing on breathing, imagining expansion, and feeling compassion, but I don't choose any of those. I just want to sit here and enjoy the moment.

I feel like I'm in a good place. I think back to how the summer started. I recall putting my VR goggles on to play *Just City* for the first time. I think about my erroneous understanding of things and everything that has happened since then. I don't feel ashamed... I actually feel compassion and love for myself. Not just myself as a child, but the current me and the version I was at the beginning of the summer. I think I know how I want to live in the future: like this. As soon as the timer rings on my phone, I get up and walk to my large whiteboard. I erase an old program flowchart and two cartoon figures from my winter semester and cover the board with writing in green marker as the words just effortlessly pour out of me:

I am my connectome—my brain network. There is no "will" that is free from physics and biology, no "soul." If I were born into a different family, with different genes, my connectome would be different, and I would be making different decisions and ending up in a very different situation. At the same time, my connectome constantly chooses its subjective values and courses of action. So here they are.

1. I choose to be kind. No natural (or supernatural) law tells me this. Humans simply get to choose which world they want to live in. My understanding of the fact that I am just my connectome helps me feel humility and compassion for others. Because it could have been me. Always. *I also choose to feel compassion for myself when things are tough. And when things are good, I choose to replace the feeling of pride with gratitude because... hello?*

2. I also choose to seek truth and base my actions on objective truth. The reality. Whether I like it or not. This is what reason and rationality *mean to me now. The scientific method is the pursuit of this objectivity. Beliefs in the supernatural (soul, god(s), afterlife, synchronicities, telepathy, etc.) are understandable but have no evidential basis. The burden of proof lies with those who make such claims. Such beliefs can easily lead to injustice due to their subjectivity, against which rationality and facts are helpless.*

I look at what I've written and realize that the second value, about reason and seeking the objective truth, is necessary for the first value, kindness and compassion. So, Grandma is right, you don't have to choose between being compassionate and being scientific; you need both. You need reason (scientific thinking) to see things as they (most likely) are, objectively. Then, if you choose justice, fairness, and kindness toward sentient beings as your values, you can pursue your "worthy goal" in alignment with reality.

At the very top of the whiteboard, where there is some space left, I summarize in three words, in large font, LOVE AND REASON.

I get dressed, make myself a veggie sandwich, and look at the whiteboard again. I feel great about this. Kind of proud—ha! As I snap a picture with my phone, I get a call. Tim from the alternative medicine center asks me how I'm doing and whether I have time to go over the letter of collaboration. I look at the whiteboard and understand that my life credo can simply remain beautiful, perfect theoretical words on the whiteboard, and something to ponder about during meditation, unless I act on it. I take a deep breath.

"Tim. I'm so sorry. It may sound disappointing, but I chose an evidence-based medical center as the main startup collaborator instead. I did some studying over the past weeks, and I know, for example, that the flu season is coming. I really want to be able to offer vaccines and things like that to the homeless people, and I know you are against vaccines and many other things, and I just wouldn't be following my principles..." I look at the white-board. "...if I do otherwise. I think the scientific method provides us with the knowledge that is as close to reality as possible." Now I feel surprisingly calm and add, "We may list your clinic as an alternative and complementary resource, but we won't be able to have a contract. I'm sorry."

"Okay," Tim replies after a few seconds. He doesn't sound thrilled, but that's understandable. "I'll let Dr. Lena know. Have a nice day. My blessing to you."

I say, "Tim, wait." I look at my first value on the white-board.

I start telling Tim about the past. About the guilt and the story with riddles. I sincerely apologize and ask him if he would be open to having tea with me to talk more about it. He agrees right away.

This feels so right. I stare at the whiteboard and smile. So, this can actually help me act in the way I choose, according to my values. It can't be that easy, though. How can I solve the funding problem for my startup with these? What am I supposed to do? To get my own money, I *need* Alex to offer me the job and pay the advance, but it looks like it's not going to happen. Wait a minute... "To get my own money, I *need* Alex to offer me the job," I replay in my head and look at the whiteboard. What on this board says I have to get my *own* money? I've been so fixated on the idea that I have to do it without help from my family that the idea of talking to my parents was not even an option. I don't know why. Or maybe I do know why. Because I wanted to prove I was a grownup. But Grandma says being a grownup is this... what I'm doing... and not necessarily doing everything on my own. I chuckle. It looks like my new life motto gave me a totally different angle on my problem. I get my phone and video call my mom. "Mom, can I ask you for something?"

"Of course!" she replies eagerly, sitting down at a desk in the study.

"Do you think I could borrow $4,000 from you for my startup project? If possible, without telling Dad until I hear about the results of the startup competition," I add quietly, hoping Dad is not around. I still prefer to show Dad my success, not the struggle to get there.

"I would be so happy to lend you the money," Mom replies and then turns around at the sound of an opening door.

"Nathan, this is a surprise; how are you? What's going on?" Dad walks into the study and joins our call right away.

Well, what can you do? I explain my request to Dad and even tell him what the startup will be about. I hold my breath and look for his reaction.

"Great. Do your thing, Nathan," Dad replies after a moment of quiet.

"Really? I thought you wanted me to come home and work for you."

"As a backup option, yes," Dad replies. I feel surprised and relieved. He adds, "I'm proud you are showing initiative and sound determined to work hard on it."

After the conversation, I repeat Dad's words in my head: "Do your thing." I wonder if he wished the start-up were for something else—not for helping the homeless—but didn't say anything. Maybe. But maybe that's just his priority: As long as I work hard, all is good. I chuckle.

In the afternoon, when I leave the office early after finalizing my report and sending it to Alex for our discussion the next day, I feel carefree. My parents support my endeavor, and I know what to do. I'm heading to Magnus University for Grandma's big presentation. I go early just in case my help is needed with the VR stations or anything. I decide to walk, as it's nice and warm outside, but not too warm. It's sunny. As I'm about to cross Market Street, a familiar figure with cool sunglasses and a typical smirk appears across the wide street on the other side of the crosswalk. For a moment, I hold my breath. Jack. It's been several months. Should I consult my life principles to choose how to react to him? No, I don't need that. It's not like I must analyze everything according to the principles every time, I probably will internalize them. Or not. I just go with the flow, and when the light turns green, I realize I'm standing still, waiting for Jack to cross to my side. It's funny how it's a risky social move, as he might not want to talk with me, and I would be stuck on this side, having missed the green light.

As Jack approaches, the words of the meditation teacher pop up in my head. *Everyone is me in disguise...* Jack joins me on my side of the road, and we, in agreement, step away from the stream of pedestrians.

"How are you? How is stuff?" I ask Jack.

"Well, the startup didn't work out," Jack replies. I don't know exactly what it means but realize I'm feeling a bit sad for him, even though he ditched me. He takes off his sunglasses and slowly says, "Dude. I'm sorry about that. About going in without you. And about the other thing." I know the other thing is what he did back in the Geniuses Club. He continues, "It made sense to me back then. It doesn't anymore."

I feel so connected to Jack at this moment, and though I don't say anything, I slightly nod and just look straight into his eyes.

Jack continues, "How are you? Any ideas?"

Without planning for it, I just start sharing. "I'm actually planning to submit a proposal on Friday for 'Street Angel'—a solar-powered tablet for the homeless to connect with volunteers, clinics, housing programs, shelters, and food banks..."

To my surprise, Jack doesn't say it's stupid.

"Who will pay for it?" he asks.

"The city. They have dedicated funds to help the home-lessness problem."

"Is it scalable?"

"Any city that sees the results would want it," I say confidently. "I researched it, and almost every city has a fitting program or a grant mechanism."

We both pause for a minute.

"I would need a partner on that," I continue. It feels good, and it feels right to say that. Maybe because deep inside, I always pictured him by my side in all this. Jack's smirk is back, and I say with a smile, "I'll send you the draft of the proposal tonight, co-founder."

Jack looks enthusiastic but slightly hesitates. "I haven't done anything for it."

We are both silent for a moment, deafened by a firetruck passing by.

"Do you have like 15 minutes now?" Jack asks after the firetruck is gone.

I look at my phone—still half an hour till Grandma's talk.

"Let's go get some user feedback," Jack says.

I follow him a few blocks away from Market Street. We approach a middle-aged homeless man sitting at the corner who, to my surprise, greets Jack with a handshake. Jack introduces us and asks Andrew, the homeless guy, to give his opinion on Street Angel.

I give Andrew a brief description of the idea and receive surprisingly constructive feedback. He tells me how incredibly hard it is to get a job if you are homeless (for starters, how about you need a permanent address even to be considered). So he asks if maybe, in the future, our startup could have a literal jobs program where homeless people could do training to learn how to service the tablets or other entry-level positions. Maybe they could do the training right there on the tablet. Andrew also says that the tablets could have a bright color or unique shape so that everyone knows what it is, including the police. In the end, he says I can ask him any other questions in the future if I need to. "You know where to find me. On most days," Andrew says to me and nods, indicating that he is usually at this corner.

Before I must run to Grandma's talk, Jack and I agree to meet the following day to finalize the paperwork before the deadline. Jack also briefly explains what had happened with his startup application. Shortly after submitting it, he was downtown and ran into a big group of people setting up a street chess tournament. He decided to join, and after several too-easy games, he faced a terrific player with a fascinating game style. It was Andrew. Jack won the tournament but stayed long after it was over to keep playing with Andrew. As they were parting, Jack was shocked to find out that Andrew was homeless. An unlikely friendship emerged, and Jack withdrew the startup application under which he would've developed a shopping cart tracking system to ensure people like Andrew didn't steal them.

"Just one thing," Jack says before we part, "Street Angel is lame."

"What?"

"We need a less lame name, maybe *StreetPal* or something. You know, like PayPal?"

"Ah! Agreed!" I laugh, realizing that I'm totally on board with it.

We do the "lame fist bump" just like we used to, laugh, and part ways. All the way from there to the university, I can't help smiling. I missed hanging out with Jack.

Chapter 29

As I approach the big amphitheater-shaped auditorium, I hear the muffled sound of the Twenty-something song. I feel emotional remembering how I teared up watching the music video. The thoughts of the vicious cycle of poverty and crime cause a heavy sensation in my chest. The talk must have already started, but people keep sneaking in through the doors into the packed auditorium. I find a seat at the back, near the cameraman.

Grandma is wearing a burgundy dress that makes her straight posture look even more perfect. In how she enunciates the words, I can hear confirmation of how much all this matters to her—the workings of a powerful life motto.

Grandma introduces the veil of ignorance concept at the heart of the *Just City* game. "In John Rawls' words, he looked 'for a conception of justice that nullifies the accidents of natural endowment and the contingencies of social circumstance.'"

She talks about the random assignment of different characteristics—which I remember doubting during my horrible rounds—using the real-life statistical data available for the U.S.

"Some of the probabilities are not independent, which is accounted for: for example, parents' social status and health." She doesn't go into details, but I assume being poor correlates with poor health. "We also used real-life national and international statistical data for events during the game due to the interactions between the player's characteristics and the laws and regulations they choose. For example, one in every three black males born in the U.S. today can expect to go to prison at some point in their life, compared with one in every six Latino males, and one in every 17 white males, if current incarceration trends continue." I can't help but shake my head; it's so messed up.

Grandma continues, "However, changes in criminal justice regulations—that can be done by the player under the veil of ignorance—are modeled as an increase or decrease in these disparities. Testing the real-life accuracy of such modeled effects is challenging, but the player's contemplation is the game's primary purpose." I think that this primary purpose was achieved in my case. That contemplation hasn't ended either.

Grandma shows examples—screenshots and short video clips from the game—and explains how the game works in detail.

"You may notice that we are trying to create a really immersive environment—and don't forget that things feel more real in VR."

That they do, I think to myself.

"You'll be able to test this at our demo stations after the presentation. We are in the process of conducting a pilot study with one hundred participants playing the Just City game for four weeks, basically four lives. The participants are college students. We haven't analyzed or published the political views data yet, but we have gained helpful insights regarding the game itself. Most participants found it very engaging—well, not without complaints either."

I feel like Grandma looks at me, although I think I am sitting too far for her to realistically see me with the dimmed lights.

"By the end of the year, we plan to analyze the data on the changes in the political views of the players."

I remember taking the questionnaire a second time after playing the game. I was feeling so down, and there was a lot of confusion in my head. I remember noting how difficult it was to answer the questions, unlike the first time. The ease of "strongly agreeing" with some statements was gone, like "Those who can pay should have access to better medical care" or "It is a waste of time to try to rehabilitate some criminals"... I wonder how exactly things changed.

Grandma continues, "John Rawls predicted that the veil of ignorance experiment would result in people choosing according to two principles: 1) Equal liberties for all citizens and 2) Permitting only those social and economic inequalities that work to the advantage of the least well-off members of the society. We hypothesize that we will observe such a shift in our participants."

Grandma moves to the next slide showing a coordinate system titled "The Political Compass." The four quadrants are colored in red, blue, green, and purple.

Someone in the audience raises a hand, and a person with a microphone goes to him. I guess they accept questions now.

"Your game sounds nice but aren't you pushing youth in the direction of the Soviet Union, with all this 'equality' rhetoric? We all know how that went!"

Grandma waits for a few seconds and replies with a soft smile, "Thank you for your perfectly timed question. As you can see on this slide, the answer is 'No.' This 'Political Compass' shows how one can understand different political orientations. Instead of the overly simplified 'right vs. left,' the Political Compass deals with both the economics and the social dimensions. The x-axis ranges from economic left to economic right, and the y-axis ranges from extreme authoritarian on the top to extreme libertarian on the bottom."

Grandma uses the clicker, and a bunch of faces with names appear all over the coordinate system of the Political Compass. Not all of them are well-known to me, but I try to find one familiar figure in each quadrant: Stalin in the top left (red) quadrant, Thatcher in the top right (blue) quadrant, Gandhi in the bottom left (green) quadrant, and Ayn Rand in the bottom right (purple) quadrant.

While Grandma explains how their hypothesis for Rawl's veil of ignorance experiment, and therefore the *Just City* game, is that it will move people toward the green (Gandhi) quadrant and away from Stalin's authoritarianism, I think about my own path. In my life, have I traveled a lot over multiple quadrants? Maybe starting in the green one, with my naive childhood dreams to help all Corduroys of the world, which may have been my childish view of equality? Although I didn't think much about justice and fairness back then, it was just a wish to help. I probably became very "purple" over time, once convinced that "unjustified" kindness cultivates laziness in people and that if you *think* about it, you will understand that, for example, it's that person's fault if someone is homeless, etc. But now I know that if you *really, really think* about it, it's not...

More questions follow, and as the host asks for one last comment or question, I raise my hand.

"I want to comment as one of the study participants who has played the game." Many heads turn back to look at me. "It was one of the worst experiences in my life." The audience becomes entirely silent. "But I think it was extremely important to me, and maybe with better prompts and guidance, I wish every young person could play it. The game has changed me. It made me understand how different other people's lives can be from mine, and it made me question what I truly deserve. Thank you, Grandma," I add to disclose my potential bias.

Grandma's face lights up with a smile, and applause follows. Many people pour down the amphitheater to talk to her one-on-one. Many others line up at the VR stations to try out the game demo session. I walk through the crowd to exit, and once outside the auditorium, I see Mark near another entrance. He is holding roses in his hand, hiding them behind his back. It's not typical for people to give flowers to professors at such lectures; maybe that's why he feels awkward. Did she call him? Did she really talk to him because of my advice? I wonder... I decide not to go up to him but nod and smile from a distance and head out of the building.

Did Grandma listen to me? I feel impressed that she probably does see me as a grownup with a valid point of view. I feel good about it and happy for her. And maybe a tiny bit envious. What is it like to find your soul mate? Or, to be more accurate, your "mind mate?"

Epilogue

I sit and meditate at home before going to the Food Bank. It's been two months since Jack and I won the Startup Incubator competition. My college classes are intense, and after lectures, and during weekends, Jack and I work very hard on our startup. We don't hang out with Adam and Jocelyn much.

Jack and I do not talk about philosophical stuff—such as values or free will—but he does his part of the job really well, and we have a lot of fun! However, I keep an eye on him. I don't want him to steer us in the old "rational" direction, but he never tries. I wonder what changed him. Was it that homeless guy, Andrew? I wonder if he reminded Jack of his chess teacher, whom he admired so much. Once I heard Jack talking to a guy from the Incubator about homelessness and saying, "It *can* happen to *anyone*."

We work on the technical part—the tablet's software—simultaneously with the fieldwork, consisting of tons of conversations (or attempted conversations) with homeless people, social workers, and many other stake-holders... It's not easy at all, but every night I go to bed exhausted and excited at the same time. I still sometimes manage to go and volunteer at the Food Bank, just like I'm planning to do today.

I finish the meditation and open my eyes. I look at the whiteboard. It still says LOVE AND REASON... Next to the whiteboard, in a frame, is the shiny Startup Incubator award that makes me smile. I also framed the two main reviewers' comments.

"The evidence-based and timely proposal addresses a tremendous pain point of our society in a uniquely creative way..." reads one of them, "...only someone truly compassionate and understanding could have conceived of this idea." Not pride—because, hello! —but gratitude and joy fill me when reading these lines.

I feel grateful for so many people and events. Grandma's *Just City* game started it all... And her undervalued Critical Thinking course... She says she wasn't successful in applying for funding to implement it in high schools. They don't get it. She needs a good marketing team or something. Every politician—oh man, everyone—should play *Just City* and take the course. How about that? If my startup one day becomes successful and I get some free time, I'll write a story about my experience and what it meant to me, and how it changed me. Grandma can then use it to promote the game and the course. People dig real stories.

In the huge building of the Food Bank, I feel at home. Dance music is playing in the enormous hall of what used to be a brick factory. Today's supervisor, Nick, assigns me to package pasta into one-pound bags. With his broad smile, he points at a free spot at a long table. A group of mainly younger people are sealing bags there. I am given the task of weighing the noodles.

I look at the crowd. I have a theory about people volunteering here. No judgment at all, but I think half of the people come here because they really want to help those in need. The other half—mostly high school students—do it for their resumes, which is totally fine! Just some time ago, I would have been in that second category. Nothing wrong with that, and, hey, people change.

Most people at my table seem to belong to one group of friends, students who are likely from the second category. A brunette girl in front of me seems not to be with them and is a little older, maybe my age. She has dark brown eyes, like those of the woman in the painting in Grandma's office. She dances a little to the music playing in the background, sealing plastic bags with a hot press.

I feel this quiet but intense feeling of joy to be alive and surrounded by these people, joy from *doing my thing*.

Nick, the supervisor, is giving his motivational speech to the volunteers:

"On weekends, we are joined by our youngest volunteers. They don't differ much from us adults except they are three times faster! Altogether, we provide 184,000 meals in our city. Daily! What a great opportunity to help your community and chat with great people!"

"What do you want to chat about?" the brunette girl asks me laughingly.

"How about free will?" I reply.

"Or lack thereof?" She smiles a wide and sincere smile.

At the same time, an estimated 7,980 other non-magical but humanly meaningful coincidences occur in the universe.

The End

Acknowledgments

I want to thank everyone I have ever met, interacted with, agreed with, or disagreed with. As Chuck Palahniuk said, "Nothing of me is original. I am the combined effort of everybody I've ever known." It becomes even clearer if you look at it from the connectomics perspective.

I want to thank K.C. Karr, my book coach and developmental editor, for her immeasurable contribution to this work. K.C.'s genius questions and suggestions shaped this story, and her coaching brought me here to a completed book.

I want to thank Kim of 100 Covers for the amazing book cover design.

I want to thank my editors, Grace Brown, Jennifer Dean, Alyssa Kruse, and Dr. Vonda, for their wonderful help.

I want to thank Lisa Cron for her genius book, *Story Genius: How to Use Brain Science to Go Beyond Outlining*.

I want to thank my husband, Ricardo Lemos, for his love and support and the extremely helpful discussions, comments, and ideas incorporated into this book.

I want to thank my personal assistant, Caron Barks, for her super helpful edits and much-needed encouragement.

I want to thank my sensitivity reader, Matthew Broberg-Moffitt, whose precious input made a huge difference in what became of StreetPal.

I want to thank my beta readers, Zira Takahashi, Lesley Dooley, Jonathan Pagel, Gonçalo Puga, Carol, and Angela Jakary, for their invaluable input.

I want to thank Suleiman Ocheni, Alexa Whyte, Kristina Marija Vella, Kim Stear, James Scott, Nathan Herring, and Brittany Beville for helping improve the manuscript.

I want to thank Brian Berni for his outstanding help in bringing this book to the reader.

I want to thank my sister, Iryna, and my friends, Johannes and Anna, for all the important discussions about life.

I want to thank my "writing buddies" and friends, Angela, Prasanna, and Kay—it was always so much fun to write together!

I want to thank Professor Sandel for his mind-blowing introduction to the philosophy of John Rawls in his freely available course of lectures titled *Justice*.

I want to thank Professor Novella for his course on *Your Deceptive Mind*.

I want to thank Professor Sapolsky for the phrase that became the key message of this book.

I want to thank Wayne Brittenden, the creator of the Political Compass.

I want to thank Jamie Woodhouse, a community builder for Sentientism, for beta-reading the book, providing terrific comments, and discussing the idea of how the veil of ignorance thought experiment might work if the veil also obscured species.

I want to thank my students who discussed the notion of free will with me.

I want to thank all my friends with supernatural beliefs. Please stay my friends.

I want to thank anyone who may be looking for their name on this list—you deserve an acknowledgment, and it is not made explicit purely for technical reasons.

I want to thank you, the reader, because that's the whole point.

Pledge

Kyiv, Ukraine

I'm writing this in August of 2022, as my home country is under a brutal, inhumane, and unjustified attack by Russia.

I pledge that as soon as the royalties from this book reach $5,000, this money will be donated to support the Armed Forces of Ukraine.

Thank you for making your contribution to this goal.

If you'd like to make a direct donation, you can do it here:

https://bank.gov.ua/en/news/all/natsionalniy-bank-vidkriv-spetsrahunok-dlya-zboru-koshtiv-na-potrebi-armiyi

A small Favor

Can I ask for a favor?

I hope you enjoyed *Just City* as much as I took pleasure in writing it for you to read.

Your feedback helps me provide the best quality books and helps other readers like you discover great reads.

It would mean the world to me if you took two minutes to share your thoughts about this book in a review. You can leave a review and/or email me your honest feedback.

Just click this link to leave an honest review. Note that you may have to sign into Amazon along the way, depending on how your device is set up.

https://www.amazon.com/review/create-review/?ie=U TF8&channel=glance-detail&asin= YOURASIN

My email: just.city.book@gmail.com

Made in the USA
Columbia, SC
19 January 2023